SOUL-WRECKED

MESSY HEARTS #2

CHARITY PARKERSON

--Warning: This book is intended for readers over the age of 18.

Copyright © 2020 Charity Parkerson
Editor: Hercules Editing & Consultants
Photographer: Dan Skinner
ISBN: 978-1-946099-67-9
All rights reserved.

Two men made weary by life. A vow to accept each other as they are. Together, they're building a beautiful future... no matter what anyone thinks.

When Jason moves to Vegas to start a new life, the first friend he makes is in the same boat: new in town with only business acquaintances to call friends. Jason is immediately drawn to the bitterness Raiden doesn't try to hide. Since he's lived his life forced to tell lies, Jason doesn't hold back with Raiden. He dumps all the truth and ugliness on him the first time they meet. No one is more surprised than Jason at

Raiden's acceptance of a criminal past that would send anyone else straight for the hills.

Raiden is used to men chasing him. After all, he gets paid because of his looks. Despite Jason literally chasing him down in a parking lot, Jason is different. He doesn't expect Raiden to smile, be quiet, and look pretty. Jason has something unique Raiden can't resist. Raiden can't explain why he keeps letting Jason deeper into his life. All Raiden knows is, he can't withstand another loss. He needs Jason to be exactly who he claims to be, because Raiden is too weak to fight against life any longer.

When two men with equally broken lives come together, no one trusts their love as real. Not even them. Someone will have to be the first to challenge the odds, or they'll miss out on a lifetime of happiness.

ONE

Sweat ran down Raiden's face. He was so fucking tired. He had been going nonstop for years now. As much as he traveled, partied, and performed every sexual act imaginable, none of it was for pleasure and he felt it. Life was aging him. He could feel the minutes flying past him at three times the pace of a normal life. He needed to finish this workout so he could get ready for his next job. Of course, Raiden couldn't remember if he had unpacked yet from his last weekend with a client.

When he had moved from Austin to Vegas, Raiden had told himself he would slow down. Take fewer jobs. Unfortunately, he hadn't thought about how sitting still gave him time to think. Things weren't at all what he'd expected. He needed to keep moving.

"Are you giving up already? If so, other people are waiting."

The muscle head who tossed the question Raiden's way wore a smirk that dug its way beneath Raiden's skin and raised his hackles. Raiden pulled out his most practiced apologetic smile.

"I'm sorry for holding up the machine. I had chemo today, and it zaps my strength. I'll just wipe it down and you can have it."

The smirk disappeared, replaced with a deep discomfort. "Um, sorry. No worries. I'll check back in a little while."

Raiden rolled his eyes as the guy turned away. He hated people. A sexy rumble of laughter washed over Raiden. His eyes automatically sought the owner of the delicious sound. A blond guy with more tattoos than skin sat nearby on the leg press. His light green eyes swam with mirth.

"I guess he'll think twice about his words before being a smartass next time."

"Probably not," Raiden said with a small smile.

Another rumble of the devil's laughter fell from the man's full lips. "Yeah. Probably not."

Raiden forced himself to move. He needed to do

something else with his eyes than stare at the walking, talking thirst trap sitting across from him. Raiden wiped down his machine, losing himself in the dread of another client. In a few short hours, he would smile and be beautiful. Right now, he didn't feel any of that and no one was paying him to pretend, so he didn't.

"I'm Jason, by the way."

Raiden's gaze slid back toward the tattooed Adonis. "Raiden," Raiden said, immediately dismissing him again.

"That's different."

Raiden suppressed a sigh. He didn't look Jason's way. "That depends on where you're from."

"Where are you from?"

Even though Raiden knew Jason referred to his obvious Asian lineage, he wasn't in the mood to play. "Texas."

"I guess I meant, where were you born?"

Raiden looked Jason's way with a barely suppressed eye roll. "Texas."

The guy's cocky smile didn't falter. "Where were your parents born?"

Raiden's inner smart ass rose to the surface. "Duoyishu."

"Oh. China."

Okay. He had Raiden's attention. Raiden softened. He flashed Jason a small smile and headed for the locker room. Through a quick shower and change, Raiden's mind kept drifting back to the hunky tattooed dude with the too cocky smile. That one was a heartbreaker. He probably had countless people scattered across the country who thought his name and smiled. More likely than not, he had never been told no. Despite his best judgment, Raiden's gaze still slid toward where he had left Jason behind as he stepped outside the locker room. The leg press was empty. It was for the best.

With a shake of his head, Raiden made his way to the parking lot. It wasn't like he had time for a man, nor would any man want him if they knew anything about him. Sometimes, it was best not to dream. He almost made it to his car.

"Raiden. Hold up."

Raiden turned. The Adonis jogged across the parking lot. His smile grew as he reached Raiden. "Damn. I didn't realize how tall you are. It's rare for anyone to match me in height." That was the only way they matched. Otherwise, they were total opposites.

"Did you need something?"

4

"Your number," Jason answered without missing a beat.

"Why?"

Jason shrugged. "I'm new in town and I think you're hot. Let's get dinner."

His confidence was something to behold. "What does being new in town have to do with anything?"

"You can show me around."

Raiden snorted. "I moved here a month ago, so I'm not who you should entrust with that chore. As to dinner, you don't want that either."

A line appeared between Jason's eyebrows. "Why not?"

"Because people usually pay me to go out with them," Raiden answered honestly. There was no sense in playing games. Raiden mentally braced himself for the rejection.

Jason's expression cleared. "Oh. And?"

Some fucked up sense of challenge rose inside Raiden. "And, they usually pay me a lot more to fuck them."

Jason shrugged. "I boosted cars for a living before I moved here. Everyone needs to work."

A chuckle burst from Raiden. "Are you being serious?"

"Completely."

He was. Raiden could see it in his eyes. Self-preservation disappeared. "I have to work tonight."

"Then have lunch with me tomorrow."

Raiden sighed. "Fine. Let me give you my number, but don't say I didn't warn you when you get pissed because of what I do."

Jason's smile didn't lose an iota of triumph. "Don't worry. I already know I live in a glass house. Plus, it's just lunch. What's the harm in that?"

Raiden had a feeling Jason could cause a lot of damage in an afternoon. He supposed he would learn soon enough. Raiden dug out one of his business cards and passed it Jason's way. "Ignore the number on the front. That's the number for the company where I work. My cellphone number is on the back."

Jason eyed the card. "Cubs for Rent." His gaze swept down Raiden's body before returning to the card. "I wouldn't call you a cub." He flipped the card over. As Raiden watched, he dug out his phone and dialed the number. Raiden's phone rang in his gym bag. Jason hung up. "There. Now you have my number too. I'll text you later and we can make plans."

Jason took a step backward toward the building. He winked before turning to walk away.

Raiden stole the chance to check out his ass. Very nice.

"Hey, Jason."

Jason stopped and turned Raiden's way. "Yeah?"

"Nice ass."

Jason roared with laughter before jogging back inside. For some reason Raiden couldn't explain, he was smiling like an idiot as he climbed inside his car. He shook his head. What an unexpected day it had been so far. He hoped it stayed that way. God knew, Raiden could use a damn break from reality.

***

ICONIC STYLIN' RIDES HAD GIVEN JASON A second lease on life. From the day he was born, Jason had been no more than a tool his dad could use to keep up his addictions. Jason paid for his dad's motorcycle shop, drug habit, and his mother's alcohol addiction with his blood and tears. Then the owner of Iconic had offered him a legit position in customization at his shop nearly two thousand miles away from Jason's parents. Since loyalty to the family had been his first life lesson, Jason had almost declined.

Then Jason had spotted a strange car in his

brother Nash's driveway. After running the tag number and doing some snooping, Jason realized his brother had fallen in love. Terror had choked Jason from that moment. Everything he had done to set his brother free was in danger of falling apart. Jason knew if his dad found out about Nash's man, Nash's life would be over. So Jason had been forced to set a new plan in motion to keep his brother safe. First, he made sure River moved Nash somewhere new. The final step had been accepting Cruz's offer to come work for him in Vegas. So here Jason was, setting the only person who had ever loved him free. It was harder than Jason expected, but Nash was in good hands with River. They would be married soon. Nash was worth twenty of Jason. Nothing mattered anymore.

Jason adjusted his respirator mask as the boss he had just been thinking about slipped inside the paint booth. A bright smile lit his face as he took a look at Jason's work. "Wow. You never cease to amaze me." Cruz's blue eyes sparkled with good humor. Everyone liked him. It wasn't hard to see why. The dude was hot—like cover model sexy— and had money to burn. Of course, Jason had always been partial to tattoos. Cruz had those in droves.

Cruz's gaze locked on Jason. "You're doing great. Seriously. You fit right in here."

Jason thanked god for the mask hiding his face. Heat beat at his cheeks. Even though he had been staying with Cruz until he could find a place to live, exposure to the guy's constant praise hadn't made Jason any less uncomfortable with it. No one had been proud of him before taking this job.

"Thanks." Even Jason heard the discomfort in his voice.

Cruz chuckled. Even that was sexy. It was truly wrong for one person to be so much. "I know. You don't like it when I tell you how good you are, but that's just me. I appreciate a hard worker. How are things going outside work? You learning your way around?"

Jason took off his mask. "Yeah. I found that gym you suggested and started my free trial this morning. It's a nice place."

"Cool. That's good. What about that club I told you about?"

Cruz's questions pulled a laugh from Jason. "One thing at a time. I haven't been here long."

Cruz's smile grew. "I know. I just want you settled. Until you're entrenched in the town, I won't be convinced you plan to stay."

Jason nodded. "I get it. I'm not going anywhere. In fact, I have a few leads on a place to stay."

"Meh. You're welcome to stay with me as long as you need. I've got the space."

He did. Cruz's house was awesome, but Jason felt weird living with his boss. Jason felt like he always had to be on his toes. Still, he couldn't let Cruz think he was ungrateful. "I know, and I have to admit it's a lot pricier here than I expected. Especially if I want to stay close to work, which I do."

"Angling for a raise already, huh?"

Jason snorted. "No. You've been more than good to me. I just think I'll probably need a roommate or something."

Cruz nodded. "Yeah. Cost of living here is a bitch, but the benefits are plenty. Like I said, though, don't rush. Crash at my place. Save your money. It's cool."

"Thanks again for everything."

Cruz slapped him across the back. "No problem. I'll let you get back to work. Check out that club. You'll thank me later."

With a nod, Jason pulled his mask back on and got back to work. Maybe he would check out the club Cruz suggested. He had a lunch date tomorrow, but tonight, he was free. Jason didn't relish another weekend of hiding in the bedroom he had been assigned at Cruz's. He wasn't the kind of guy who sat home alone, but he also didn't really know anyone here. Jason's mind drifted back to the parking lot of Grid Iron and the sexy man who liked Jason's ass. A smile pulled at Jason's lips. Wow. Raiden matched Jason in height, which meant he had to be at least six-three, but his features were feminine. Sculpted cheek bones. Full lips. His hair was bleached blond and his eyes a sweet brown. He had the longest and sexiest legs Jason had ever seen on a man. Raiden was stunning.

Jason had never been one to care about anyone's sex. He loved men, women, and anyone transitioning between the two. Jason didn't care about any of that. He just loved sex. Dirty, uninhibited, and raw sex. Raiden practically screamed carnality. Jason wanted him from the first smartass comment to that rude gym rat, and Raiden was only one phone call away.

Jason set his stuff aside and moved to the corner of the paint booth. After a minute of struggling with his coveralls, he got his phone out. He couldn't call. Someone might hear and know he was on his phone instead of working. That left sending a text.

Jason: *Do you go by Raiden all the time? Or do*

your friends call you Raid or Den? Something in between?

Raiden: *It's always Raiden. What about you? Are you always Jason? How about Jace or Son? LOL.*

Jason smiled at his phone like an idiot. He didn't care. No one could see him, and life had not been good to him.

Jason: *I'm always Jason.*

Raiden: *Really? Because I saved you as nice ass in my phone.*

A snort escaped Jason. It was much louder than intended and echoed in the enclosed booth.

Jason: *I've smiled more since meeting you this morning than I have in months. Please tell me you still plan to see me tomorrow.*

Raiden: *Even though my good sense is screaming that you're trouble, yes. I still plan to see you tomorrow. There's a Greek place on Sandcastle Lane. How about we meet there at noon?*

Jason: *Greek sounds great, but how about I pick you up on my bike?*

Raiden: *I'm too tall to ride a boy's handlebars.*

Jason: **snort* I meant my Harley.*

When Raiden didn't respond right away, Jason almost risked calling him. He worried he had slipped too far into bad boy territory with the request. Just when he almost gave in, his phone buzzed.

Raiden: *1130 Greystone Way. Noon.*

Jason: *I'll be there.*

With a smile stretching his lips, Jason shoved his phone back in his pocket and got back to work. If Jason had known life would be this much brighter in Vegas, he would have ditched his family a long damn time ago. His smile fell. He wished he could call Nash and tell him he was right. It was too bad Jason hadn't moved to Vegas before he had lost the only person who cared about him. Hindsight really was twenty-twenty. It was too late now to take anything back. All Jason could do was look ahead.

TWO

HE SHOULDN'T HAVE ACCEPTED THIS DATE. THAT was the only thought that kept bouncing around inside Raiden's head as he fended off another crotch grab. While it wasn't unusual for men to try for more than company, and it was also true Raiden had done more for the right price, this was different. Raiden's sixth sense was screeching at him, pounding at his brain, and warning him to run. Only the fact that they were still inside a crowded nightclub kept Raiden from taking off. Plus, he needed the money. It wasn't that Raiden was broke or desperate. He didn't want an unhappy client destroying his reputation and damaging future funds.

"Bring my doll another drink," James yelled at a nearby server.

Since they were in the VIP section, and the guy wanted a tip, he smiled at James' yelled demand. Raiden recognized the guy's smile. It reflected the desperation of a low-paying job coupled with catering to the spoiled rich. Raiden almost pitied him, except he wasn't the one getting molested.

With a practiced shy smile touching his lips, Raiden deftly swept James' hand away from his ass and held on to it to keep it busy. "Are you having fun?"

James swept a leering glance down Raiden's body, taking in the tight black dress and heels he had requested. "I could be convinced to have a better time." He patted his knee.

Raiden obediently sat.

James ran his fingertips down Raiden's spine. "You really are a work of art. Those long legs make men dream."

Raiden pretended to look away as if embarrassed. In his head, he gagged. It wasn't that James was a bad-looking guy. He was rich and smelled good. None of those things masked the disgusting pig inside him.

"Vodka Collins," the server said, appearing beside him. He handed the drink directly to Raiden. Their gazes met. An understanding passed between them. They could not let James touch his drink. The drink was also more ice than alcohol. Additionally, the server had shoved a slice of lime and a few cherries in the glass, making it impossible for there to be much liquor. It seemed everyone noticed the handsy James. The drink was gone in one gulp, but Raiden pretended to keep sipping so James wouldn't order another. His gaze skirted the club. He counted the minutes in his head. Raiden knew down to the second how much longer he had to endure this. Not every client was like this one. In fact, Raiden had several regulars who were nice men. Some were older and lonely. Other were introverts who liked intelligent conversation occasionally. A few were ultra-elite with sexual quirks they didn't want to become public knowledge. Raiden didn't hate this life. He had gotten to travel to places he would have never seen and been able to afford things he never would have otherwise. This career wouldn't last him forever, but he had no regrets, and he played things smart, setting himself up for an uncertain future.

James swiped up Raiden's thigh, attempting to slip beneath the hem of his dress.

Raiden came to his feet. It was time to slip away. He flashed James a smile. "Excuse me. I need to run to the restroom."

The way James's eyes flashed had a hint of fear sparking in Raiden's gut. He wasn't sure of that look. Either James knew Raiden planned to run or he thought Raiden had just invited him for a bathroom tryst. Either way, Raiden was fucked.

Ruby Redd's was every bit the experience Cruz promised it would be. The place was an eclectic mix of high-class nightclub and everyone-is-welcomed bar. A huge dance floor filled one side of the room with a DJ booth at the back. Straight couples and same-sex couples danced alongside one another. The VIP section was a roped-off corner with velvet curtains partially hiding the uber rich from everyone else. After getting his ass grabbed twice, Jason found a spot in the corner at the end of the bar where he could put his back against the wall, drink, and watch the crowd. He was two sips into his first beer when his gaze landed on a familiar face.

It was almost funny. Jason had only met Raiden one time and the guy still stood out like a diamond among coal. Of course, the fact that he wore heels that put him six inches above the rest of the crowd was another reason Raiden couldn't be missed.

Whatever the reason for Jason's gaze to land on Raiden, he hadn't looked away since. Raiden was uncomfortable. His open discomfort made his every line seem stiff. But goddamn, he was beautiful. If Jason had thought about it, this was the perfect look for Raiden's features. He had the body of everyone's dreams. Jason's mouth watered.

Raiden sat perched on a guy in an expensive suit's knee just inside the VIP section. The guy was every bit of two hundred and fifty pounds of solid muscle. He kept leering at Raiden in a way that made Jason's skin crawl. Every time the guy touched Raiden, Jason's gut tightened a little more as Raiden's spine visibly stiffened. Everything about the situation felt wrong, from Raiden's tense expression to the worried looks everyone around them kept shooting their way. Jason fought the urge to cross the room and put his fist in the guy's face. It wasn't jealousy driving Jason. Raiden looked scared and repulsed. Jason wanted to save him, but it wasn't his place.

Still, as Raiden flew to his feet and the guy came to his, Jason straightened away from the bar. Even from across the room, Jason could see the indentions in Raiden's arm as the guy grabbed it and held on. They headed for the door. Even though Raiden didn't struggle, his expression was openly panicked. Jason headed their way.

A blond woman stepped into his path. She barely reached his chin, but she still blocked his exit. "Hi."

Jason fought the urge to shove her aside as he tried keeping an eye on Raiden. "Nice to meet you. Got to go." He stepped around her, but he wasn't quick enough to reach Raiden before he disappeared out the door. The crowd slowed him. He stepped on toes and elbowed a few people before finally making it to the door. As the cool night air washed over him, he took a breath and scanned the parking lot. Thankfully, Raiden was tall as hell. He spotted Raiden against an expensive sports car, refusing to get in. With his back pressed to the car, the guy tried again to jerk Raiden by his arm and shove him into the car. When Raiden only slid about a foot but didn't bend, the guy invaded his space and tried to kiss him. Jason started running, headed their way. Before Jason could reach them, the guy snapped when Raiden turned his head, rejecting him. Everything seemed to slow—like Jason could see everything happening in slow motion, but he couldn't reach them in time. The guy who outweighed Raiden by nearly a hundred pounds punched Raiden three times in the face so fast, Jason almost didn't see the hits. Raiden crumpled.

A roar rose in Jason's throat as the guy moved to scoop Raiden from the ground. "Get away from him, motherfucker."

The guy turned his way, looking unfazed. Before he could try again to kidnap an obviously unconscious Raiden, Jason was on him.

"Mind your goddamn busi—"

Jason snagged the guy's hair, yanked him forward and down, until he could knee him in the face. He felt the guy's nose break. Jason wasn't satisfied. All he could see was red. He had been dealing with bullies his entire life. Jason had been beaten until the edge of death by grown men when he was no more than a tiny child. He had been shot by his father. Stabbed twice and countless things he could never discuss. This guy might be bigger, but he wasn't crazier or meaner. Plus, Jason had literally nothing to lose. Jason landed several blows to the guy's ribs, savoring the cracking of ribs beneath his fist. He might have spent every second until the police arrived, doing his best to kill the guy, but Raiden stirred.

Jason shoved his prey away. "Get the fuck out of

here, and if I catch you coming around him again, you're dead."

Dark brown eyes latched on to Jason with hate. He spit blood in Raiden's direction. "You can have the whore."

Jason's feet automatically shuffled his way, determined to make the asshole pay for insulting Raiden. Raiden gasped in pain and Jason couldn't see anything else. He bent and scooped Raiden from the ground. As he lifted Raiden into his arms and held him against his chest, Jason's heart skipped a beat. He was so light and fragile. Blood seeped from two cuts on his face. His lip was split and there was a gash beneath his eye. With Raiden's attacker forgotten, Jason hurried to his truck. His door automatically unlocked as he reached the passenger side. Jason fought to get the door open without setting Raiden aside. A hand reached around him and opened the door. Jason's gaze shot the new arrival's way. It was the blond woman from inside.

"Thanks." Even to Jason's ears, his voice sounded gruff.

She shrugged. "It's no problem. Sometimes the helpers need a little help too. It's Allison, by the way. Now it really was nice meeting you." She walked away before he could thank her again.

"Are you stalking me?"

Jason's gaze shot to Raiden's face. His eyes were open and fixated upon Jason's face. He looked lucid but in pain. In spite of everything, Jason still smiled at the sight of his gorgeous eyes. "Maybe I am."

Jason gently set Raiden in the passenger seat and buckled his seat belt. "Don't go back to sleep, okay? I don't know where the closest hospital is."

"No hospital. Just take me home, please."

Jason eyed Raiden's cuts. "Are you sure? You might need stitches and you really should press charges."

Raiden shrugged. "Nobody cares about people like me. I'll get some of those butterfly things or whatever."

Jason nodded and closed the door, but he had every intention of convincing Raiden to get help. As he circled the truck, he noticed the large crowd they had drawn. A few people were on their phones. Jason knew he had to get the hell out of there before the cops showed up. He did not want to be on the local police radar here. Jason had moved here for a fresh start. It wasn't until he was halfway down the road that he realized his knuckles were split and bleeding and there was blood all over his clothes that didn't belong to him. He pulled into the first twenty-four-hour pharmacy he spotted, backed into a parking spot, and dug his first aid kit out from the backseat.

He dabbed at his knuckles with an alcohol pad and caked them in antibacterial cream, hoping to stop the bleeding. Jason was in the zone. He was on such familiar ground, trying to clean up a mess of blood and hide the evidence, that he almost forgot Raiden was there until he peeled off his shirt. Bare-chested, he dug through the back, looking for something half-ass clean to don long enough to make a quick supply run. Raiden's fingertips skimmed down Jason's ribs as he leaned over the seat. Jason's eyes fell closed. He took a cleansing breath. His gaze moved Raiden's way.

"Thank you."

Discomfort had Jason giving a sharp nod and looking away. He found a shirt and pulled it on. "I'm going to run in and find some of those butterfly bandages and whatnot. Don't move. I'm locking you in so no one can get to you, but I'll hurry." When Raiden didn't respond, Jason found himself looking the guy's way again. Even bleeding and broken, he was the most beautiful man Jason had ever seen.

It was obvious Raiden had been waiting for Jason to look his way. He held Jason's stare without blinking. "I'm not afraid. I know you'll take care of me."

Jason's throat swelled without warning. He felt Raiden's belief in him. His trust. Jason wouldn't let him down. With a nod, Jason slid from the truck and headed inside. He kept his head down, trying not to draw any attention to himself as he grabbed bandages, pain relievers, and an ice pack. Before making it to the self-checkout, he spotted a cooler with drinks and ice cream. Jason grabbed a few of both and quickly checked himself out without meeting anyone's stare. He made it in and out in record time. As he climbed back behind the wheel, he found Raiden trying to clean away some of the blood on his face.

Jason quickly peeled off his shirt again and handed it Raiden's way. "Here. Use this. It's no loss."

Raiden hesitated.

"Seriously," Jason said, trying to soothe him. "It's okay. You're more important than a shirt."

After a moment, Raiden reluctantly accepted. He held the shirt against his cheek and closed his eyes. Jason stole another moment to stare at him. Some strange form of overprotectiveness rose in Jason's chest. He needed to keep this one safe. Jason forced his eyes away and started the truck. He had searched Raiden's address earlier, making sure he could find the place for their lunch date, so he felt semi-confident he could get there without Raiden pointing the way. Then he would take care of Raiden. Jason would make him better.

Numbness coated everything. Raiden wanted to feel something. Outraged. Humiliated. Scared. Nothing touched him. Mostly, he was just tired. He didn't realize he had dozed off until Jason touched him. Jason unbuckled Raiden's seatbelt, making him realize he was home. He spent a moment confused about how Jason knew where he lived before he remembered texting Jason his address earlier. Jason started to lift him from the truck.

Raiden waved off his efforts. "I can walk."

Concern etched Jason's features. "Are you sure? You don't weigh a thing. I don't mind carrying you."

His sweetness made Raiden's eyes sting. Sometimes, he forgot there were good people in the world. "I'm good." As Raiden swung his legs out the door, his body almost made a liar out of him. After a moment of dizziness, he took off his heels before trying to stand. When he didn't drop, Raiden took a slow step toward the door. His head still felt a little fuzzy, but he did okay. Jason stayed at his side, casting him worried looks all the way to the door. Once there, Raiden had to take a slow breath to clear his mind before he could type in his code to disengage the lock on his front door. It beeped, letting him know the door was unlocked. He let Jason inside and headed for the alarm before typing in the same code.

"You shouldn't have the same code on your alarm as your front door. It makes it way too easy to break in."

Raiden ignored the lecture. He needed to sit down. Without a word, he headed for the couch. He dropped. His gaze found Jason. Jason cast a look around the room before focusing on Raiden.

"Let me grab the stuff I got from the store from the truck and I'll be right back."

Raiden watched him go, wondering if he really would be back. He could slip away now and disappear from Raiden's messy life. Raiden wouldn't blame him if he ran. Jason returned too quickly to have considered it. If Raiden's lip didn't hurt so badly, he might have smiled at the way Jason immediately made himself at home. He shut the door, reset the alarm, and headed for the kitchen.

Raiden heard the fridge open and close. Jason rummaged around before returning long enough to hand Raiden a soda and two pills. "Take that."

Raiden didn't have the heart to tell him he didn't drink sodas. He did as told, trying not to wince at the too-sweet flavor, as he watched Jason move from room to room, inspecting each one. Jason disappeared inside the hallway bathroom for a second before heading into Raiden's bedroom. In a detached sort of way, Raiden realized he should probably care that an admitted thief was prowling through his house, looking at everything he owned. Raiden cared not at all.

Jason reemerged a few minutes later and came for Raiden. "I've got you a bath started. Let's get you cleaned up."

This time, Raiden didn't argue as Jason lifted him into his arms. It felt good against Jason's bare chest. He truly was a work of art. His entire upper torso was covered in tattoos. He wore his masculine beauty as if it meant nothing. Raiden wondered what it would be like to be him.

At the edge of the bathtub, Jason set Raiden on his feet and immediately began stripping him. Raiden absently wondered if he should stop him. No fucks rose to the surface. For the first time in his life, a man stripped him with no lust in his eyes. Raiden couldn't look away from Jason's face. While Raiden imagined he looked a mess, and Jason had seen him get knocked out, which wasn't the least bit attractive, Jason didn't look at him like everyone else. Raiden's entire life had centered around his looks and men being attracted to them. For the most part, that fact had brought him nothing but pain and grief. It was strange watching Jason undress him with as much respect as possible. He didn't directly look at Raiden at all until Raiden sat submerged in hot water and bubbles.

Jason rolled up a towel. "Lean your head back on this," he said, urging Raiden to rest his head on the towel on the edge of the tub. "I want to clean up these wounds."

Raiden leaned back. He had to bend his knees to slide down enough to do as Jason instructed. While he had bought a nice home on the outskirts of Vegas, with a gorgeous bathroom, he was taller than the world typically accommodated. Raiden stared up at Jason's face while Jason wet a washcloth and gently washed his face. Jason winced several times, as if he took Raiden's pain into himself. For a moment, Raiden wondered if he truly had that power. Raiden still couldn't feel a thing.

"Is there anyone I can call for you?"

Raiden didn't completely understand the question, but he knew he had no one. "No."

"You should've let me take you to the hospital. It's likely this cut under your eye will scar."

Despite knowing he should care, considering his job depended on his looks, Raiden couldn't work up any concern. "It's fine."

Jason nodded as he patted Raiden's face dry. He pulled a bandage from his back pocket and went to work on putting butterfly stitches on the cut. When he finished, Jason sat on the floor beside the tub and gave Raiden his full attention. "How are you feeling?"

Raiden crossed his arms over his chest and relaxed. "I don't know. Thankful you're here, I guess. I'm sorry you got dragged into things."

"No one dragged me. There's no way in hell I would stand by and watch anyone get hurt. That's not who I am. Countless people, including my own mom, stood by while terrible things happened to me. I would never do that to anyone else."

Raiden wanted to know all his stories. He felt less alone in that moment than he had in years. "Tell me about it. I have time and need the distraction." Raiden's teeth chattered on the request in some form

29

of fucked-up delayed adrenaline rush or panic attack. Whatever the cause, Raiden needed Jason to find him something else to focus on.

Jason added more hot water to the bath as he gave Raiden what he needed. "I was born in a small town near Destin. I have four older brothers, but I was only raised with one, Nash. I don't have any contact with the others. My dad was a drug addict who beat us. My mom is an alcoholic, so she was usually passed out or oblivious. Nash tried keeping me safe. He took a lot of horrible abuse to spare me. When I was eleven, we got busted stealing a car. Nash was fourteen, and he told the police that he was only babysitting me at the time, so I had no idea the car was stolen. He took the blame for everything. I let him. He took the fall and got sent away. Little did I know, he was the lucky one. I was left alone with my dad." Every word Jason spoke was delivered without an ounce of feeling. Considering his current position, Raiden completely understood locking emotions away. Sometimes, that was the only way to hang on to sanity. "I learned pretty quick that it was easier to do whatever my dad said. Nothing mattered but feeding my parents' addictions. I did what I had to do to survive until I lost myself for a while." Jason shrugged. He set his elbow on the edge of the bathtub, propped his chin up with his hand, and held Raiden's stare. "Now Dad is dead, Nash is getting married soon, and I'm here. I don't have a place to live, but I have a job, and—for the first time in my life —I'm free."

Jason's openness loosened some of Raiden's locked down emotions. "I used to feel free. When I first started this job," he clarified. "Growing up with eleven siblings and immigrant parents, we were dirt poor, and I never had anything that wasn't handed down. Then I went to work for Cubs for Rent, and I had money to buy and do whatever I wanted for the first time in my life. I traveled and paid cash for a new vehicle." He held Jason's gaze, wanting him to understand. "There was nothing I wouldn't do for the right price as long as I didn't have to go back to being poor." Raiden admitted something he never had. "I think I paid with my soul."

"What happened tonight wasn't your fault."

He was sweet, and wrong, but mostly sweet. "In high school, I was dead set on becoming a nurse. I chose my pathway, filled out all the paperwork to be a candy striper, and had it all planned out." Raiden stared at nothing as he spoke, seeing nothing except his youthful ignorance. "Except I didn't account for how poor we were and how no one had time to drive

31

me around to fulfill my volunteer hours and no one could afford for me to go to nursing school. Every day, I watched my dreams get smaller and smaller."

"It's not too late. You could still go to nursing school."

Raiden's gaze locked on to Jason. Reality was very real now. "I no longer care to save anyone. Tonight was no different than a dozen other nights. I only see the faces people keep hidden. I don't matter enough for people to hide their rot with me."

"I'd like to say that not everyone is like that, but I don't know too many good people either." Jason stood and moved to the bathroom closet, making himself at home. He came out with a huge, thick towel. "Come on. Let's get you dried off and I'll put you to bed. You look ready to pass out."

Raiden released the plug to let the water out of the tub and stood. His gaze stayed locked on Jason's face as Jason scrubbed him dry before wrapping him in the towel and plucking him from the tub. Raiden let everything happen to him. He didn't have the strength to argue. Jason carried him to the bed and gently sat him on the edge. He looked almost reluctant to release him.

"What do you usually wear when you sleep?"

Raiden peeled off the towel, tossed it in the

direction of the clothes basket, and crawled beneath the covers. He didn't give any fucks about Jason openly watching. Not only was Raiden not the least bit modest, Jason had seen and dried it all already. There already was no pride between them.

Jason turned off the lights and sat at Raiden's side. "Roll over."

Always the obedient one, Raiden rolled onto his stomach.

After ensuring he was completely tucked in, Jason started lightly rubbing his back. "Go to sleep. No one will hurt you with me around."

A lump grew in Raiden's throat. Even before he had been left alone in the world, no one had been there for Raiden the way Jason was now. Raiden couldn't let his efforts go to waste. He closed his eyes, let his body relax, and pretended to sleep. It was the only way he knew how to show appreciation for what Jason had done tonight. After all, no one had ever stood up for him before now. Raiden appreciated it more than Jason would ever know.

EVEN ONCE RAIDEN'S BREATHING DEEPENED, Jason didn't move away right away. He couldn't stop watching over Raiden. There was only one place Jason had seen the level of bitterness he saw in Raiden's eyes: in the mirror. Jason had never experienced this level of kinship with anyone. He desperately wanted to fix things. Raiden looked delicate and fuckable. Jason swiped his hands through his hair and stood. There was an undeniable hunger in Jason's gut. Jason looked down at his hands. His split knuckles held his attention. He fought the urge to get back in his truck and find that bastard who had dared to touch Raiden. The rage was real and eating him, because Raiden was unbelievably sexy and that didn't give anyone the right to touch him without his permission. Jason's hatred of men who thought they had rights they didn't ran deep. He needed to fix this.

Jason headed for the living room and whipped out his phone. He dug through his wallet, finding the card Raiden gave him. With no real plan other than feeding his fury, Jason dialed the number on the front. It rang four times, making his anger grow with each unanswered ring.

"Cubs for Rent. This is Tucker."

"What kind of two-bit shit show are you running there? I just had to save one of your employees from getting kidnapped and probably raped from one of your so-called clients. Don't you protect these people at all?"

"Which one of our guys? Is he okay?"

Jason checked the face of the card. While Raiden wasn't a common name, he didn't want any misunderstandings. "Raiden Li."

Tucker hissed. "That's terrible. He's such a sweet guy, and he's already had such an awful year. I can't imagine." He blew out a breath. "Okay, well, while we can't go on every date with everyone listed on our site, we're still here for him. Let me check which client it was real quick." There was a pause and Jason could hear the guy clicking keys. "James Renault. All right, I'm blacklisting him now and booking a flight to Vegas. We'll take care of any hospital bills and get the paperwork started for a restraining order."

"He wouldn't let me take him to the hospital." Even Jason heard the gruffness in his voice.

Silence met his words. Finally, Tucker sighed. "That's not surprising, I guess. Just tell him to keep any receipts for his care and we'll reimburse him. One of us will be there by morning. I'm sorry this happened. We'll fix what we can."

Since Tucker sounded genuinely concerned and

had a plan, Jason was somewhat mollified. "All right. I'll let him know."

Before he hung up, Tucker stopped him. "What did you say your name is?"

"Jason Hayes."

"Is Raiden okay?"

Jason blew out a breath. His heart beat faster than it should. "Yeah. I guess. Likely both eyes will be black by morning. He has at least two cuts that should've had stitches. I put butterfly stitches on them since he wouldn't let me get him help."

"It sounds like he's in good hands. Thanks for calling and keeping us appraised. I don't imagine he would've called if you hadn't and that's why we're here."

Jason nodded without thought. "Thanks for trying to do what you can. Talk to you later." He likely wouldn't, but Jason didn't know how else to end this unfortunate conversation.

"Yep. Have a nice night."

Jason disconnected the call and stared down at his feet. He was tired now that the adrenaline had worn off. Part of him thought he should probably go home, but he didn't want to leave. His chin lifted. Raiden had one hell of a house. It wasn't huge, but it was nice, and Raiden was nice, and Jason felt fucking useless. He turned, trying to decide what to do. Raiden stood quietly leaned against his bedroom door frame. Only a thin white robe covered him. It stopped just below his ass. Jason didn't know how long he had been standing there or how much he had heard, but he knew Raiden made his mouth go dry. Jason had never been thirstier in his life.

He decided to stick with current circumstances rather than his badly timed lust. "Tucker says someone will be here by morning and they're blacklisting the client."

Raiden gave a small nod. Without a word, he straightened away from the door, crossed the room, and took Jason's hand. "Come on. You look exhausted."

Even though Jason's feet moved, he still argued. "I can go home, if you want."

"I don't want." At the edge of the bed, Raiden dropped the robe and climbed back into bed. He held the covers up for Jason. "I promise I won't molest you."

A smile tugged at Jason's lips. He set his phone on Raiden's nightstand and slid into bed beside Raiden.

"Are you sleeping in your jeans?"

"It's for the best," Jason said while trying to

breathe through his mouth to keep from inhaling Raiden's sexy scent that lingered on the sheets.

"Sounds horrible." Raiden draped one leg over Jason and scooted closer. Jason automatically lifted his arm so Raiden could cuddle against his chest. It was murder. Raiden had one of those long sexy legs across Jason's waist and Jason couldn't act on the desire that crippled him. "You're not at all what I expected when you asked me to lunch."

Jason smiled into the dark at the quietly spoken words. He needed the distraction Raiden offered with his claim. "What did you expect?"

He felt Raiden shrug. "That loud guy who grabs your ass, tells you to move out from in front of the TV, and tells all his friends you're just a friend."

While Jason's first instinct was to joke that maybe he was that guy, he couldn't. "I can't imagine anyone claiming you as just a friend. I'd be honored for anyone to think you're with me. You're way out of my league." He really was. Jason was homeless, for fuck's sake. He was no one's catch. "Also, I don't have the attention span to watch TV."

"Warning noted."

Jason tilted his chin down and tried to read Raiden's expression. "What's that supposed to mean?"

Raiden didn't flinch. "I likely won't hold your attention long. It's okay."

"People are different from television shows," Jason said, refusing to get upset. Raiden didn't know him. No one did, really. "Shows are flashing lights and gimmicks. People have depth and secrets. Every single person has a side of themselves they show no one. I like trying to read people and find that side."

Raiden's hand smoothed across Jason's stomach, reminding him of all the lust he had tried forgetting. "I like that you're more than I expected. Maybe tomorrow, I'll look more appealing than what you've seen so far."

Jason tightened his hold on Raiden. "If you get any more appealing, I might not survive the blood loss to my brain."

To Jason's disbelief, Raiden shifted positions and swept his hand down Jason's body until he shaped Jason's erection through his jeans. Raiden settled back down in Jason's arms like nothing happened. "I was about to call you a liar, but dang." Raiden sounded genuinely surprised.

Despite the crazy situation he was in, Jason couldn't stop smiling. "I have an extremely beautiful and very nude man in my arms. What did you expect to find?" Even Jason heard the laughter in his voice.

"Well, I mean, I'm kind of a mess, so..." He shrugged. "It's not like you were throwing off any signals. You haven't tried to kiss me or pet me. I don't know."

An exasperated sigh escaped Jason. "I'm not about to paw a guy who just got attacked. While I can't control what my dick decides to do, and I might be a lot of things, I'm not that big of a piece of shit."

Raiden kissed his chest. It was a sweet, lingering press of lips against Jason's skin. "I think you're amazing. I'm glad we met."

Jason skimmed his lips across the top of Raiden's head. "Get some sleep, beautiful."

Raiden's grip tightened for a moment before he relaxed. Jason stared at the bedroom ceiling and soaked up the heat of Raiden's body draped over him. His muscles relaxed. He should have been uncomfortable, but he wasn't. Things should have felt awkward, but they didn't. Jason felt oddly at home for the first time in his life. Sleep came a hell of a lot easier and faster than he ever expected.

THREE

Despite his physical discomfort, Raiden felt more at peace than he had in a long time as he trailed through his house with a cup of coffee in his hands. He told himself he simply didn't feel like sitting. The truth was he couldn't stop checking on Jason. On his side, with his head resting on his arm, Jason slept peacefully. A smile pulled at Raiden's lips as he came to stand in the bedroom doorway for the tenth time. Jason took up too much room and looked out-of-place in between Raiden's delicate sheets with his huge muscles and tattooed skin. He looked like a giant wicked boy. Raiden swallowed past the lump growing his throat. He was Raiden's hero.

The doorbell rang, startling Raiden. He rushed

to the door, hoping the noise didn't wake Jason. A quick check of the peephole showed Tucker on the other side. He quickly disarmed the alarm and answered. A huge smile lit Tucker's face as the door opened. It fell at the sight of Raiden.

"Damn, sweetie. How are you feeling?"

Raiden shrugged and stepped aside so Tucker could step inside. "Meh. I've been better. I've been worse. You really didn't have to come all this way."

Tucker cast a look around as he spoke. "Sure, I did. I can't let someone get away with hurting one of our guys."

Raiden led Tucker to the kitchen, hoping they would be far enough away from the bedroom they wouldn't disturb Jason. "Would you like some coffee?"

Tucker nodded and grabbed a chair at the small kitchen table. "Please and thank you."

Raiden set some sweetener and creamer on the table and moved to pour Tucker a cup. He eyed the giant guy who was one owner of Cubs for Rent. He was one part of identical triplets. Tucker was huge and nice. He was also the only brother Raiden ever dealt with, so he didn't know if he could tell the triplets apart. While all three had the same dark hair and green eyes, Tucker just bled kindness. He stood out to Raiden.

Raiden set the cup in front of Tucker. "Here you go."

Tucker flashed him a smile. "I guess I should have fixed my own coffee. You look terrible." He winced. "I didn't mean that how it sounded."

A chuckle slipped from Raiden. "Don't overthink it. I saw myself in the mirror this morning. It looks worse than it feels. Jason took good care of me right away. Otherwise, I probably would've felt worse today."

"Jason is the guy who reamed me out last night, right?"

Raiden tried hard not to smile, since it hurt, but Jason made him feel important. Every time he heard his name, he felt warm on the inside. "Yeah. I guess he was a little upset."

"That's understandable." Tucker pushed some papers Raiden's way. "I just need your signature on a few things, and I'll make sure that rat bastard James can't get within five hundred feet of you ever again."

Raiden snagged the papers, quickly flipped through them, and signed every line at the bottom. He didn't give a single fuck if there was some hidden jargon, signing away his legal right to money or whatever. Raiden didn't care about any of it. If anyone had bothered to ask, he would have told them he had stopped giving a damn about everything, including himself, a long time ago. A movement in the doorway caught Raiden's eye. Jason hovered, looking worried he wasn't welcome.

Raiden fought against the smile that pulled at his cut lip. "Good morning, hottie. Did we wake you?"

Jason's gaze slid Tucker's way for half a second before landing on Raiden and not moving. "No. I don't usually sleep this late. I guess I was extra comfortable."

Raiden motioned Tucker's way. "This is Tucker Kodiak. He's one owner of Cubs for Rent."

Jason gave Tucker a quick nod as he crossed the room and came to stand over Raiden. He tilted Raiden's chin up and turned his face from side to side, inspecting his wounds. "The ice pack I bought should be nice and cold by now. It might not do any good now, but it might numb your face."

Raiden felt kind of warm and fuzzy with Jason taking care of him before acknowledging anything else. "It doesn't hurt."

"Good." Jason kissed the top of his head and then focused on Tucker. "You're who I talked to last night, right?"

Tucker stood and shook Jason's hand. "I am. Nice to meet you."

Jason didn't return the sentiment. "What's the scoop on James?"

Tucker didn't look offended. "I've already talked to the police this morning. A detective might stop by sometime today or tomorrow."

"I'll be scarce for that."

Raiden chuckled at Jason's retort. He focused on Tucker and explained on Jason's behalf. "Jason beat the shit out of him."

Tucker's expression shifted, closing. "Oh. That complicates things a bit. James might want to file counter charges."

Jason shrugged. "He can want it all day, but we didn't exactly exchange information."

"He's not getting any names from me."

Tucker scrubbed the spot between his eyes and sat. "Okay. I'll do what I can. James is a professional fighter, so he might not want any bad publicity. That could play in our favor."

Raiden made a dismissive gesture. "Honestly, Tucker. I don't give a damn about any of this. You've blacklisted him as a client. That's good enough. If getting a restraining order is too much work, then don't bother. A piece of paper won't magically make the guy a good person. In fact, it might only make things worse."

He didn't look happy about Raiden setting him free of this chore. "Of course, it's up to you, but I would prefer for you to have that piece of paper. Do you really want to limit where you can accept dates so you don't run into this guy anywhere?"

Raiden shrugged at Tucker's question.

Tucker looked like he was biting his tongue hard enough to taste blood. Raiden fought the urge to look Jason's way for advice. Tucker finally sighed. "Moving on." He pulled a check from the pile of paperwork and passed it Raiden's way. "Toby, Tanner, and I would like you to take two weeks off to recover. Based on your rates and usual bookings, this should cover your losses for the next two weeks. The second check is for any medical costs that might arise. We'll handle suing James and any monetary settlement above the amount of those two checks and legal fees will come to you." Raiden listened to everything with half an ear as he eyed the checks. The first one was decidedly more than his usual two weeks of working. The one for medical fees was ten thousand. Raiden borrowed Tucker's pen again and signed the back of the second one. He held it out to Jason. "You should take this."

Jason didn't reach for it. "No, thank you."

Raiden didn't back down. "You paid for everything at the pharmacy last night, took care of me, and you were injured too. I'm not taking no for an answer on this." He set the check in front of Jason and focused on Tucker, letting Jason know the topic was settled. "I appreciate your kindness, Tucker. You and your brothers have been nothing but good to me. I'm sorry you felt like you had to fly all the way out here. I guess I should have considered that when I moved here but stayed part of the company."

Tucker looked scandalized that Raiden would even say such a thing. "This is exactly why my brothers and I started this company. We want to protect people from people like James. Don't worry about the travel. We have employees as far away as California. If we weren't willing to come to you when you needed us, we wouldn't have bothered starting this company at all. The escort business is a legitimate service. There are tons of people out there who genuinely just want someone to keep them company and no one has a right to take advantage of the people providing that service because of their own fucked-up take on what we do." Tucker was truly winding up to rant. He looked more and more outraged by the second. "While I can see you're not wanting to rock the boat, I've got no problem flipping this whole goddamn canoe. No one puts their hands on our guys. End of story."

Jason was smiling. That was the only reason Raiden decided to let them have their way. "Of course, I'm onboard with whatever action you choose to take."

Tucker gave him a sharp nod, as if satisfied with that answer. He chugged his coffee and stood. "I still have a few things left to do before my flight back this evening."

Raiden curled his nose. "You're flying in and out on the same day. Ewww."

As Tucker gathered his things, he laughed. "As you know, I have an incredibly sexy husband at home and I'm partial to my bed, so yeah. It's worth the pain of all-day travel."

That was understandable. Tucker did have an adorable husband. "I'll walk you to the door," Raiden said, starting to his feet.

Tucker waved off his offer. "No. Stay put. Relax. I can find the door. Call me if you need anything else, okay?"

Raiden nodded. "I will. Have a safe flight home."

With one final kind smile for Raiden, Tucker focused on Jason. "Thank you for taking care of

Raiden. I won't let any heat fall on you for doing the right thing."

"I appreciate that," Jason said, shaking Tucker's hand. Jason didn't focus on Raiden again until they were alone. Raiden couldn't look at anything else. The moment Jason's sexy gaze slid Raiden's way; butterflies stirred in Raiden's stomach. Jason's green eyes held him captivated. "I bought you ice cream last night. That's not much of a breakfast, but I'm not much of a cook."

A smile exploded across Raiden's lips. He regretted it immediately. "Ouch. Fuck." He felt his lip. It was bleeding again. He sighed and moved to stand. Jason jumped to his feet and pushed Raiden back down in his chair.

"Nope. I've got you." He grabbed some paper towels and wet them before snagging the bag filled with stuff he had bought last night. Jason stood over him. Raiden dutifully lifted his chin and let Jason care for him. It was nice, staring at Jason's gorgeous eyes while Jason focused on cleaning his lip and swiping antibiotic cream over the cut. With that out of the way, Jason inspected the butterfly stitches, ensuring they were still holding up. When his gaze finally connected with Raiden's, Raiden's heart sped. Jason's thumb swiped Raiden's bottom lip. He looked hungry. The air thickened. Then Jason took a step back, and the moment was over. He looked everywhere but directly at Raiden. "So, what's the plan for today? I know we were supposed to go to lunch, but I imagine you don't feel like being jostled around on my bike. Would you like me to order us something? Do you care if I run home and get cleaned up first? I don't think I have any shirts left in my truck."

Raiden shook his head. He had no idea why he made Jason so uncomfortable. "Let me grab a quick shower and we can head over to your place. From there, we can see how I feel. Maybe a quick ride won't hurt anything, but I'm definitely not up for sitting in a restaurant with everyone staring at me."

Jason nodded. "We'll figure something out."

With no real plan in mind, Raiden came to his feet. His hand slid across Jason's stomach. Jason finally focused on him again. Raiden tried for a small smile. "I promise I'm not trying to make you uncomfortable."

"I'm not."

"Good," Raiden said, moving closer. He kissed Jason's shoulder and backed away. "You just seem to be having a hard time looking at me."

This time, Jason didn't look away. "You're hurt

and I'm way more tempted to kiss you than I can control when I'm looking at you. I'm sure you know exactly how beautiful you are. You don't need me to tell you and I don't want you to think that's why I'm here."

Raiden fought the urge to ask why he was there if it had nothing to do with his looks. He didn't think he had much else to offer. Instead, he focused on being as honest as possible. "I'm glad you're here." He turned away before Jason could respond. Raiden was the one who was uncomfortable now. He wasn't used to showing his heart to anyone. If he wasn't careful, Jason would crush him.

He rushed to the bathroom. Raiden knew he probably looked like he was running away, but it didn't matter. He told himself he was hurrying so Jason could get home. No doubt Jason was tired of sitting around in blood-encrusted jeans. Raiden hadn't even realized he had forced Jason to live like that all night until Jason had entered the kitchen earlier. He took the shortest shower in history, threw on the first clothes he came to, and quickly brushed his teeth. Through every step, Raiden avoided his reflection. Even as he quickly brushed his hair and ran some styling product through it, he never looked directly at himself. By the time he re-emerged from the bathroom, Jason sat on the couch, putting on his shoes.

Jason glanced up as Raiden entered the room. He did a small double take before his intense stare stayed completely locked on Raiden. "Damn. It's like you're two different people. Last night, you rocked that sexy dress. Today, you're this drop-dead gorgeous guy from the gym. I'm not sure anyone has ever wowed me like you."

Heat rose in Raiden's cheeks. He had no idea why Jason's compliments hit so much harder than anyone else's ever had. He fought the urge to make less of Jason's words. "I'm kind of gender fluid, I guess. Like, I'm pretty comfortable being seen as a woman sometimes, if that makes sense."

Jason stood. The muscles flexed in Jason's chest and Raiden's stomach felt funny. "It makes sense. Are you ready to get going?"

With a nod, Raiden grabbed a pair of shoes and slipped them on. "Let me grab a bottle of water for the road. Do you want one?"

"Sure."

Raiden rushed to the kitchen and grabbed Jason's check. He knew Jason would try to quietly leave it behind. Jason didn't know Raiden. This money would end up in Jason's account one way or another.

He stuffed the folded check in his back pocket and grabbed their water before heading for the door again. Jason watched his every move like a hungry lion. Raiden had a feeling Jason would eventually take him down like a predator falling on his prey. Probably sooner rather than later. Raiden couldn't wait.

On the drive to where Jason currently stayed, the houses got progressively bigger as they went, until Jason turned down the gated driveway of a huge home. He pushed a button on his keys as they neared the massive detached garage and a bay door slid open, letting them inside.

"This is my boss's house," Jason explained. "He owns Iconic Stylin' Rides. He hired me to do custom paint jobs. Since I had to move from Florida to accept the job, he's letting me crash in one of his guest bedrooms until I find a place. Hopefully, it won't be too much longer."

Raiden followed him inside. The ceilings were ridiculously high, and Raiden had no idea why that was the detail that captured his attention first as they stepped through the door. The second sight to hold him captivated was the tattooed-covered shirtless dude who strode into the room as they came through the door. With messy dark blond hair and a perfect body, he looked like a rock star. His wicked-looking smile added to the package.

"Hey, man. There you are. Ruby Redd's must've been everything I promised it would be. You lost your shirt and found..." The guy's voice died as he focused on Raiden. He blinked and quickly recovered. "Hey, I'm Cruz Dalamar." Cruz switched his beer from one hand to the other, wiped his hand on his pants, and then held it out for Raiden to shake.

"Raiden Li," Raiden said, lightly accepting his handshake.

Jason motioned Raiden's way. "Is it okay if Raiden hangs out with you while I grab a quick shower?"

While Cruz's smile never lost an ounce of luster, his eyes moved from Jason's blood-covered jeans to his fucked-up knuckles to Raiden's face in quick succession. "Sure. That's cool."

With a nod, Jason focused on Raiden. "I'll be right back."

"I'll be fine." With Raiden's promise still hanging between them, Jason jogged off, as if in a hurry to get back.

Cruz watched him go. The moment he was out of sight, Cruz's smile fell. He focused on Raiden, looking intense. "Did Jason do that to your face?"

"No," Raiden rushed to assure him. "Jason rescued me from someone else. Without him stepping in to help, you might've seen me on the news this morning when they found my dead body in a ditch."

Relief etched Cruz's features. "Damn. That's good to hear. I've never heard anything bad about Jason and I didn't want to think the worst." He waved for Raiden to follow and headed for the couch. Cruz spoke over his shoulder as they went. "Are you okay now?"

Discomfort owned Raiden as they chose opposite ends of the leather couch and sat. "Yeah. It was just one of those things. This guy had too much to drink and got handsy before trying to shove me in his car. You know, the typical Friday night attempted kidnapping."

Cruz looked horrified rather than entertained as Raiden had hoped. "Did you call the police?"

"A police report was filed this morning," Raiden said, hoping that would be explanation enough. An idea hit. "So, you're Jason's boss. Could I get your help with something?" He dug the check from his back pocket. "I was on the clock last night when everything went down, so my employer gave me this check to cover medical expenses. Since I didn't go to the hospital and Jason is technically the person who cared for me, I think he should get this, but he won't take it. Being new to town, I know he could use the money."

A mischievous smile lit Cruz's face. "I like you. You're underhanded. That's a quality that's vastly undervalued." He motioned for Raiden to pass him the check. "His paycheck is direct deposited each week. I'll put this in his account and make a notation on the deposit that it's from you."

"Thank you."

Cruz winked and tucked the check in his pocket. "He's likely to get irritated."

Raiden shrugged. "He'll survive."

The way Cruz smiled gave Raiden the impression he was used to having his way. "I see we'll get along great. Would you like a beer?"

His face hurt. "I would love one. Unless you have something stronger. Honestly, I'm feeling like real shit today. Don't tell Jason."

With a sexy rumble of laughter, Cruz pushed to his feet. "Follow me. You've come to the right place for pain control." Raiden followed on Cruz's heels while Cruz kept talking. "Back in the day, before I became a semi-respectable business owner, I had many barroom brawls. Hell, sometimes I woke up with a fucked-up face and no memory of how I ended up that way." The room Cruz led him into was obviously his playroom. A pool table sat in the center of the room alongside a foosball table. Pinball and arcade games lined one wall while a fully stocked bar lined the other. It was a man cave in every way. Cruz poured him a shot of whiskey. "Here you go."

"Thank god," Raiden whispered before turning it up.

Cruz looked impressed when Raiden didn't as much as flinch as the liquor burned its way down. He poured Raiden another. He didn't look directly at Raiden while doing so. "So Jason played the hero and now you're what? Friends?" He dragged out the question, confusing Raiden.

"I suppose." He killed the second shot.

Cruz shook the bottle at him.

Raiden thought it over. "Yeah. One more."

"My man," Cruz said with a laugh, filling the shot glass again.

Raiden hadn't eaten anything in more than twenty-four hours and the liquor hit almost immediately. It was the good shit—expensive and strong. Before he could push the glass aside, Cruz filled it again. It looked like he was getting drunk today. Thank fuck. He was mentally exhausted and needed a break from himself. Raiden didn't want to stop until he couldn't feel his face and that had nothing to do with the cuts and bruises. Cruz offered him a barstool and Raiden settled in. A liquid lunch sounded like exactly what he needed.

WHEN JASON RUSHED INTO HIS BEDROOM, HE had every intention of hurrying through a shower and getting back to Raiden as fast as possible. Then he looked in the mirror. He looked like hell and he was spending the day with Raiden. Raiden was already ridiculously out of his league. Jason found himself dragging out his electric razor and trimming his hair. One thing led to another, and he was full-on manscaping. From there, the hot water of his shower felt better on his tired muscles than he cared to admit. Beating a guy's ass was harder work than he remembered. After his shower, he couldn't settle on what to wear. Raiden was really fucking with Jason's head. In the end, he just threw something on because nothing he had was nice anyway.

By the time he made it back to where he left Raiden, he was gone. Jason blinked at the empty living room. Loud laughter floated down the hall. Jason followed the sound. Pool balls banged together followed by more laughter. As Jason stepped inside Cruz's man cave, his gaze landed on Raiden first. Bent at the waist and holding on to the side of the pool table, Raiden laughed so hard that barely any sound escaped. Jason's gaze moved Cruz's way. Cruz laughed equally hard, but his focus never wavered from Raiden. While Jason wasn't the jealous type, Cruz had way more to offer than Jason did, and he openly watched Raiden like Raiden would be his next meal. That wasn't happening.

"What did I miss?"

Raiden looked up. His face was blood red and his eyes swam with laughter. "I can't play pool."

"I don't know if the word 'can't' is the word I would use," Cruz said still laughing. "Maybe 'shouldn't' is a better description. He almost took out the pinball machine. To be fair though, that might be the liquor."

As Jason crossed the room, he slammed into a wall of alcohol. He missed a step. Jason felt sure he couldn't pass a sobriety test now just from walking into their party for two. "Jesus Christ. I wasn't gone that long."

Raiden leaned heavier on the pool table than

necessary, proving how hard he fought to stay upright. He squinted at Jason. "You look adorable, though. Did you get a haircut?"

Jason fought a blush. "I might've gotten a little carried away while cleaning up."

Cruz looked between them. His expression underwent several changes. Finally, he dropped his pool stick on the table. "Well, I know when I'm beaten. I'll let you two get on with your plans for the day."

Raiden focused on Cruz. "Thank you for being my partner in crime."

Cruz winked. "Anytime. You know where I live, so you know, don't be a stranger. Next time, we'll play sober."

"Sounds good," Raiden said, keeping his gaze locked on Cruz until he disappeared. When his sweet brown eyes moved Jason's way again, his expression shifted. Jason automatically breathed deeper. Everything about Raiden was sexual. He couldn't blame Cruz for being interested. "I need you to do something for me."

"Anything." Even Jason recognized he had agreed way too fast. He didn't take it back.

Raiden's eyes flashed with devilry. "I need you to kiss me while I still can't feel my face."

Jason blinked. "Did you get drunk so I can kiss you without hurting you?"

Raiden made a dismissive motion. "I was already in pain. Kissing you without crying is just a bonus."

"Why didn't you tell me you were hurting?"

Jason's aggravation obviously didn't bother Raiden. He snagged the front of Jason's shirt and towed him closer. "You're wasting precious numbed face seconds."

Jason cupped Raiden's face between his hands, trying hard not to cause him pain. His body kept moving forward. The motion was out of his control. He needed Raiden's body against his. His feet didn't stop until he had Raiden backed against the pool table where he couldn't get away. He wanted Raiden a little too much. Jason didn't want to hurt him. That was why he tried going slow. He lightly brushed his lips across the uninjured corner of Raiden's mouth. Jason needed to taste him. His lips parted. He traced Raiden's bottom lip with his tongue. Raiden gasped and Jason tried pulling away, but Raiden wouldn't let him. Jason was helpless as Raiden covered his hands and held him in place. He was useless as Raiden's tongue curled inside his mouth and teased him into kissing Raiden deeper. Their kiss was slow. Methodical. Jason knew he was being seduced, and he was defenseless. In his life, Jason had kissed countless people. Not once had he been tantalized and toyed with the way Raiden enslaved him with his kiss. It was perfect and Jason hadn't known a kiss could be so powerful. Jason was enthralled.

Raiden pulled away and lightly kissed the tip of Jason's nose. From there, he moved to Jason's cheek. Soft butterfly kisses licked his skin while Jason stood with his eyes closed and his heart in Raiden's hands. Raiden weaved a spell over him, addicting Jason a little more with every brush of lips across his skin. He fought to lift his eyelids. When he finally managed to pry open his eyes, Jason's heart skipped a beat. Raiden looked exactly how Jason felt—like something monumental had occurred between them.

"I didn't expect to meet you."

Raiden's quietly spoken words mirrored Jason's thoughts. When Raiden had caught his eye at the gym, he hadn't expected this connection. Raiden rattled him. Made him wish he was a good man without a black past. Raiden made him want more than he ever had with anyone else.

"Can I keep you?"

The way Raiden smiled at his question melted Jason's heart. As quickly as it appeared, Raiden's smile dimmed a hair. "I'll understand when you change your mind and don't call again."

Jason stroked Raiden's bottom lip with his thumb, mesmerized by his beauty. "Why would you say that?"

"Good men always leave me behind."

A smile tugged at the corners of Jason's mouth. "You're in luck. I'm not a good man." He took a step back. "Let's get some food in you. Come on, we'll run through a drive-thru on the way back to your place and save the bike ride for a better day."

Raiden nodded and straightened away from the pool table. Before Jason could head for the door, Raiden touched his arm, stopping him. He held Jason's stare. "By the way, I love that you were obviously taking your time to look good for me. But, for the record, I already thought you were beyond sexy. You don't have to impress me."

Jason couldn't stop himself. He pressed another quick kiss to Raiden's lips. "You matter." Jason couldn't think of a better way to explain why he wouldn't stop trying to impress Raiden. Raiden was worth it. He deserved a man who tried. Jason wanted to be that man. He wanted to be Raiden's man.

FOUR

JASON HAD A WAY OF ALWAYS MAKING HIMSELF at home that fascinated and amused Raiden. After running through the drive-thru of a popular sushi place, Jason had completely taken over Raiden's home. He found a large blanket to spread across the living room floor, tossed a few pillows on top, and created an indoor picnic. Raiden sat in the center of the pillows and watched. As far as Raiden was concerned, Jason could have sat down a good ten minutes ago, but he seemed set on making things perfect to whatever image he had in mind. He found Raiden's Bluetooth speaker and set up a playlist on his phone. Afterward, he dug through Raiden's fridge and discovered Raiden preferred sparkling water over soda, so he switched out Raiden's drinks. From there, he spread their food out in some artistic pattern that mattered not at all. Raiden let it all happen, because this seemed to be important to Jason.

"Do you ever feel out of place?"

Jason froze halfway through creating a sheet roof over Raiden's head, using Raiden's kitchen chairs and second best sheets. He looked thoughtful. "No. Not really." He went back to building Raiden a fort. "When I was a kid, my parents would go to these drunken biker parties where everyone got high and had a big orgy or whatever. Nash and I would be stuck, entertaining ourselves in strangers' homes while trying not to draw too much attention to ourselves. Nash would build us a blanket fort in the back of Mom's station wagon. He always brought a little penlight and books so he could read to me or we could color. Back then, I loved those nights, because I had the best brother. He was my only friend. Then I got older and realized I should've been terrified. Those blankets were to cover the windows so no one would see us and hurt us." Jason paused and stared at nothing for a moment, making Raiden wonder what he saw in his mind. He shook his head and finished his fort. "Nash always did a damn good job of acting like he wasn't scared—like it was just a good time for him too. Now, when I think about it, he must've spent every second sick with worry. He never got enough credit for putting up with me. I guess that doesn't matter now," Jason tacked on absently as he finally settled down across from Raiden.

"Why doesn't it matter now?"

Jason rearranged the food again, avoiding Raiden's stare. "Because Nash is done with me. You should try the Rainbow Roll first. The guy working the drive-thru said it's the best."

Raiden waved off the suggestion. "I know. I was there. Why is Nash done with you?"

A sad smile touched Jason's lips. "Too many reasons to name, if I'm being honest. I knew he was all I really had, and I took more than I gave until I used him up. It doesn't matter. Try the Rainbow Roll."

Truthfully, Raiden wanted to push. He wanted to keep asking questions and demanding answers, but he didn't like the way Jason visibly hurt, so he ripped out his own heart to save him. "I shared a bedroom with three younger brothers. It was horrible." Raiden chuckled as he made the confession. His smile fell. "But it was also kind of awesome because we would talk late into the night, making our momma fuss. It was impossible to be lonely or cry without a sympathetic shoulder. I moved out the second I turned eighteen, but I still thought we would be friends forever. Despite my hatred of being poor, we were all very close." Raiden's chest hurt. "I suppose, when it comes to siblings, you never know what you have until they're gone."

"Did your siblings cut you from their lives too?" Jason smiled, as if the question had been a joke, or the thought of anyone cutting Raiden from their life was ridiculous. Raiden wished he hadn't started this conversation.

"They're dead."

A line appeared between Jason's brows. "All three of them? What happened?"

"All of them, period. My whole family," Raiden said with a sweep of his hand. "I'm the only one left." He took a breath. The pain was almost numbing now. It was as if, at some point in the past year, Raiden had stopped being able to feel. Maybe his heart had shut down to save his sanity. Either way, he didn't feel the sting. He felt nothing. "A massive flood took out the electricity in their area. They were running a generator to keep warm and carbon monoxide filled the house while they slept." Raiden made another sweeping gesture. "They were just... gone." Raiden picked up a Rainbow Roll and took a bite. He chewed without looking at Jason and without tasting a thing. With nothing left for him in Texas, Raiden had moved to Vegas, hoping to heal. Instead, he found himself turning a little harder every day. He wasn't sure he liked himself any longer or cared what happened to him. Raiden was equally baffled why Jason was there. Raiden had nothing to offer. It was only a matter of time before Jason saw it too. But, for now, Raiden had to accept the company Jason offered. Maybe they both just needed someone to be there.

WITH HIS THOUGHTS RACING, JASON FOUGHT FOR what to say. Apologizing seemed empty. Moving on, like Raiden said nothing, seemed cold. He wished he was better with words. Jason wished he was better, period.

"I bet Nash would know what to say right now,"

Jason said without thought. Raiden's gaze finally moved his way again. Jason held his stare and kept going. "You'd like him. He's a good person. I mean, I know there's nothing anyone can say that would change anything, but I feel like he would know how to comfort you better than me. He would know how to make you happy." Jason rubbed his arm. "Truth be told, I'm pretty useless."

To his surprise, a small smile appeared on Raiden's lips. "You built me a fort. I think you're pretty fucking amazing." His shoulders heaved as he visibly took a deep breath. "Let's stop being depressing. I don't know about you, but I'm ready for something good to happen. Let's shake this conversation up. You just moved here, and it's time for a new life. What are you looking for as far as living arrangements go?"

Jason wished this topic was better, but really, it wasn't. He had no idea when or how to get out of his current circumstances. "Well, I'd love to find a place that isn't an hour's drive from work, but I'll probably need a roommate if I stay close to the shop. Vegas is a lot more expensive than I imagined."

Raiden picked at his food and asked questions between bites. "Where is your work located?"

He had to picture the town in his head before he

answered since he was still learning his way around. "About ten minutes from here. It's off Winston."

"What are you looking to spend a month on rent?"

Since Raiden sounded confident and focused, Jason was honest, hoping he had some leads. "I can't go more than a thousand. Otherwise, I won't be able to afford to have any sort of life. I figure, if there's two of us, that gives us two thousand a month."

Raiden nodded, looking thoughtful. "Yeah. You could probably find something in this area for two grand a month. Possibly. Can I offer you a different solution, though?"

Jason shrugged. "I'm all ears. You've been here longer, and I really don't want to live with my boss forever. He's awesome, but he's still my boss."

"Yeah. You can't be yourself in that position," Raiden said, hitting the nail on the head. "You should move in with me." Raiden held up a hand, stopping Jason before he could turn down the offer. "Just hear me out. As you can see, I have plenty of space. You said yourself that you need a roommate, and I'm a much better option than someone you don't know. This place is paid for, so you don't have to worry I won't pay my half of the rent and get us evicted." Raiden's expression turned somewhat shy.

"I think we like each other, so no clashing personalities."

Jason didn't know what to say. When Raiden put things that way, it made perfect sense, but there were a few exceptions. "As amazing as that sounds, why would you want this? You don't need me to help pay the bills. You're doing great on your own. This seems like a step backward for you. You know my past is pretty checkered."

Raiden shrugged. "I don't see you as a step backward. My life isn't exactly ideal as far as new friendships go. I'm completely willing to accept you as you are, if you think you can do the same with me."

For a moment, all Jason could do was stare at Raiden. There was only one thing wrong with Raiden's speech. "I'm not bothered at all by your choice of employment, but I don't see you as a friend, and I can't let you think that. So how am I supposed to move in down the hall? How am I supposed to pretend I don't want more?"

Raiden's expression turned sultry. "Well, I mean, I don't need your money. So what else do you have to offer?" Before Jason could wrap his mind around the question enough to answer, Raiden motioned toward their surroundings. "Obviously, you're an amazing fort builder." His gaze moved over Jason's body. "You've proven you can keep me safe." A wicked-looking smile curved Raiden's lips. "I don't want you to pretend anything, Jason. The opposite, in fact. I'm asking you to be absolutely shameless with me."

With every word Raiden spoke, temptation rose like the tide inside Jason. He had never been very good at being good. Raiden didn't want him to behave. He wanted Jason to move his things in and fuck him like his dick paid the rent. For someone like Jason—someone with questionable morals—the moment felt a lot like he had died and gone to heaven. Jason shifted onto his knees. He pushed the food aside and moved forward, stalking Raiden. Raiden looked more than ready to have his space invaded.

Jason kept moving until he had Raiden on his back and Jason straddled his body. "I know your face hurts, even though you don't want me to know it. As much as I love kissing, that can wait, and my tongue can do other things."

An adorable laugh burst from Raiden. Jason was immediately addicted to the sound and wanted more. His gaze skimmed Raiden's body, searching for any way to steal more happiness. He shoved Raiden's t-shirt higher. Raiden must have seen something in Jason's eyes because his laughter turned to horror.

"No."

A smile exploded across Jason's face. "Oh, yes."

Raiden tried scurrying away.

Jason quickly moved lower and blew on Raiden's stomach.

Loud laughter filled the air. Raiden struggled beneath him, trying to get away. There was no mercy in Jason's heart. He blew on Raiden's stomach, making rude noises and tickling him before moving to Raiden's ribs. He used his tongue to torture Raiden, tickling him even more as Raiden fought to get away even as he screamed with laughter. Raiden managed to flip onto his stomach and slither forward a foot. Jason dropped his weight, pinning Raiden to the floor. The fort crashed down around them, covering them with sheets. Jason didn't stop. He kissed the small of Raiden's back. Raiden's laughter turned to moans as Jason reached beneath Raiden and loosened his jeans. He shoved at Raiden's pants and bared his ass. He bit and sucked Raiden's cheek. A loud pant caressed his ears. Jason didn't stop. He peeled Raiden's jeans and underwear down his long legs before tossing them aside. Jason eyed the sexy round meal spread out before him. He had never been hungrier in his life.

With one hand braced on the floor, Jason dipped his head and licked the back of Raiden's thigh. He licked upward until he reached the spot where Raiden's leg and ass met. He sucked. A moan filled the air as Raiden pushed backward against Jason's lips. Raiden's head was still buried beneath the sheet and he made no attempt to remedy the situation. Jason took advantage of the freedom to do whatever he wanted with no witnesses. It was freeing. He skimmed his fingertip down Raiden's crack. The gasp that sounded beneath the sheet fed Jason's actions. He could play all day, but then again, he couldn't because he was too desperate for Raiden.

Jason palmed Raiden's ass cheeks, squeezing and massaging before spreading them for his inspection. His stomach muscles clenched. He wanted that hole in every way he could possess it. There was a swamp of pre-cum forming in his underwear. His cock twitched to be inside Raiden. Jason needed all of him. He dove in face first. A cry bounced from the walls as Jason tongued Raiden's asshole. He licked and speared. The more Raiden squirmed and moaned, the harder Jason worked. Raiden gleamed with saliva as Jason took what he wanted, swearing the pleasure was his. He didn't move until he worried he might finish in his jeans. There weren't any clear thoughts left in his head. Need owned his every action. When his patience finally snapped, Jason sat back on his heels and dug through his wallet, desperately searching for the lubricated condom he kept inside. He threw his wallet aside when he found it. Jason tore at the front of his jeans as he ripped open the condom package with his teeth. His motions were frantic as he suited up. He couldn't recall a time he felt this crazed with passion.

With a condom finally in place, Jason snagged Raiden's hips, pulled him backward until Raiden was on his knees, and shoved his way inside. It wasn't enough. Jason wrapped his arms around Raiden's chest and towed him back against his chest. On his knees, he rocked. It still wasn't enough. His heart needed more. With Raiden pinned to his chest with one arm, he grabbed Raiden's dick and stroked. With his cock buried inside Raiden to the hilt, he pumped at Raiden's cock like it was his own. He squeezed his eyes shut and went to work. Every moan and gasp was his guide. Nothing mattered but the way Raiden's asshole tried sucking him deeper. He was transfixed by the pleasure milking him. Jason didn't thrust. He let Raiden's body do all the work while he pleasured Raiden.

Raiden reached over his head and grabbed Jason's hair. He held on while trying to fuck Jason's hand. Jason's stroke quickened. He pumped faster and faster as he moved closer to the edge. Raiden stiffened in his hold. A loud cry assaulted Jason's ears. Raiden's body convulsed, sending Jason into oblivion. He sucked air, riding out the waves as he massaged every drop of cum from Raiden. His body turned to jelly. Jason eased Raiden back to the floor as he collapsed with him. Jason rolled to one side, sparing Raiden his weight while he tried kissing every place he could reach. His heart was snagged. Jason's soul was wrecked. No one had gotten under his skin before, but he knew Raiden was there. He felt Raiden digging into his heart a little more with every second they spent together. Jason held Raiden against his chest and squeezed, hugging him.

Raiden reached behind him and caressed Jason's face. "I accept your down payment."

A breathless laugh burst from Jason. He really, really liked Raiden. If he planned to ever take a chance on anyone, Raiden was the one. "Promise me you'll tell me if you get sick of my face."

Raiden didn't hesitate. "Only if you swear to do the same."

"Deal."

"Deal," Raiden said, sounding breathless.

Like that, Jason had sealed his fate. He couldn't believe a loser like him had struck gold like Raiden. He supposed some people won big in Vegas. Jason just never dreamed it would be him.

FIVE

WHILE AIMLESSLY FLIPPING THROUGH THE channels, Raiden nearly hurt himself rolling his eyes. He hated daytime TV. He wasn't sure what kind of simpering fools TV stations were catering to, but Raiden didn't know anyone who wanted to watch anything he passed. Raiden tossed the remote aside. He had already been to the gym but didn't stay as long as usual. Too many people gave him sidelong looks because of his fucked-up face. Plus, he just wasn't feeling it today. He checked his watch. It was only ten in the morning. Raiden released a loud sigh just to cut the silence. Jason wouldn't be home for a really long time.

The truth hit from nowhere. Raiden didn't used to be like this. He used to fill his days with meaningless crap and barely notice the passing of time. Then he asked Jason to move in and boom. The very first day, he couldn't make it through a full day without watching the clock. Raiden wasn't the type of person to wait. If he wanted something or someone, he went after it. This was no different.

He grabbed his phone and searched for the address to Iconic Stylin' Rides. It really was only about ten minutes away. Raiden checked the time again. If he started on his hair and makeup now, he could be there by lunchtime. He would go easy on the makeup. Keep it classy. He only needed to cover his bruises. Raiden didn't want Jason's co-workers to think he was abusive.

He stood and ran through his outfits in his mind. Raiden knew he could be flashy without thinking. He needed to tone it down. He was headed to a legitimate business, after all. There was a light purple button down that made his eyes pop. A smile tugged at Raiden's lips. He could be respectable and desirable at the same time.

Raiden picked up the pace. He wanted to see Jason. It was possible he might be smothering the guy. In fact, he looked downright needy. Fuck it. They were likely only temporary. Jason didn't strike him as the type to settle down. Not to mention,

Raiden didn't exactly have the type of job that made him appealing. He definitely had no plans to quit. So he would steal what time he could get. Raiden would cherish every drop of excitement and happiness until it all inevitably went sour. Despite that awful thought, Raiden smiled. He couldn't wait to see Jason.

CONSIDERING JASON COULDN'T STOP SMILING like an idiot, he had never been more thankful for his respirator and corner booth. No one could see him or judge him. Seriously, he couldn't stop. He had never been happy like this. Jason didn't know how to control it. The only time Raiden had been out of his sight all weekend was when Jason had made a quick run to Cruz's picking up some clothes and whatnot. Now that Jason was back at work, he had a hard time controlling his impatience. Several times he had dug out his phone, ready to text Raiden. In the end, he put away the device without typing a word. Jason worried about looking desperate and suffocating Raiden. He felt an almost crazy level of attachment already. He was scared he would end up driving Raiden away.

Instead, the moment he got a break, he texted Nash's fiancé, River. He had promised to let River know when he found a place to live. Texting the news had the added benefit of giving Jason an outlet for his excitement.

Jason: *I found a place. It's only ten minutes from work. I'm moving in tonight.*

River: *Yay! Send me the address so I can send you a wedding invitation. Also, let me know how much it costs to fly home and back. I want to pay for you to come home for the wedding.*

A hint of exasperation ran through Jason. River was way too nice, and it was wasted on Jason. Plus, Nash would likely lose his shit if he learned River had paid for Jason to come to his wedding.

Jason: *I don't want you spending money on me. Plus, Nash doesn't want me there. The last time we spoke, he made it clear I'm no longer a part of his life.*

River: *Nash and I made the decision together to pay for your trip here. So if you're thinking he doesn't want you, you're wrong. It's not you he cut from his life. He loves you. He wants you here.*

Tears pricked at the backs of his eyes as Jason read River's message. He sniffed.

Jason: *How long do I have to save for the trip? I*

81

really don't want you to pay my way, but I also won't miss it.

River: *Six weeks.*

His mind raced. He wanted to help Raiden with some bills, but he would also love to bring Raiden with him.

Jason: *Can I bring a date?*

River: *Nash says as long as it's not your mom, that's fine with him.*

Jason snorted and switched to his banking app. He had no idea how much money he had saved so far that could go toward the trip, but he no longer needed money for a down payment on an apartment. With six more weeks, he could probably swing two round-trip tickets to Florida and a hotel. He logged in to his bank. For a moment, he stared at his balance, trying to understand what he was seeing. Jason flipped to the recent transactions. There was a ten-thousand-dollar deposit from Cruz. Jason logged out and checked his emails. There was one from the shop's accountant, notifying him of a deposit. He clicked on it. A growl rose in his throat as he read the details. He had no idea how Raiden did it, but that damn check from Tucker was now in his account.

"Hey, man. I never heard you come in last night."

Jason looked up from his phone as Cruz came

sailing into his booth. As always, Cruz wore a bright smile and had a coffee in hand. "That's because I didn't. What's the deal with you depositing ten-K in my account?"

Cruz's smile never wavered. "Raiden gave me a check that he was adamant you were owed. I just passed it along."

Jason shook his head. "I really wish you hadn't done that. I didn't want it."

Cruz held his hands up in surrender while still managing to hold on to his coffee. "Hey, man. I don't know much about much, but I know how to keep a honey happy. Let them be the boss. If he says to take the money, take the money. Disagreements get in the way of sex and that's a big nope." He sipped his coffee as if the conversation about ten grand was nothing. Jason sighed. It probably was nothing to Cruz.

He decided to drop it and focus on another topic. "Before I forget to tell you, I'm moving my things out later tonight."

"Wow. Really? You found a place already? That was fast." Cruz slapped him across the back so hard, he nearly knocked Jason from his chair.

Jason shrugged, trying not smile like an idiot.

"Raiden offered me a place, and I knew all along I'd likely need a roommate, so this works."

Cruz's smile fell. His expression blanked. "Wow. You're moving in with Raiden? As a roommate? That's..." He blinked. "That's not going to blow up in your face at all," Cruz said, dragging out the words, as if he hated to be saying them.

Jason laughed. He couldn't help it. Cruz looked ridiculously horrified and Jason couldn't work up a care. He knew how things looked and sounded. Hell, he even knew he was likely making a huge mistake, but fuck it. Life was short, and he was used to fucking up. Right now, he was happy. Jason would take it. "It won't be the first thing that's blown up in my face," Jason said, laughing harder at his own bad joke. "I'll be fine."

Cruz smiled and shook his head. "Well, if push comes to shove and you need to move back in, you know where I live."

A light tapping sound had them turning their heads toward the mouth of the booth. Raiden stood nearby, looking sexy as sin and ridiculously out of place. Both his eyes were still black, but they had taken on a yellowish hue and Raiden had mostly covered the bruises with makeup. The butterfly stitches couldn't be concealed, but overall, he looked a hell of a lot better than he had two days ago.

Raiden flashed them a smile. "Hi. The guy up front said it would okay if I came back here."

Cruz smiled like he couldn't be happier. He waved for Raiden to join them. "Of course. It's cool. Just be careful of any wet paint you see. You don't want to get this stuff on your clothes. It won't come out."

Jason ate up the sight of Raiden as he stepped gingerly inside the booth, ensuring he didn't accidentally brush against anything.

Raiden eyed the bike Jason had been working on all morning. "Wow. This is badass. I'm truly jealous of whoever is getting this bike."

"That's all Jason," Cruz said, slapping Jason across the back again. "He was a damn good investment. I have to get back to work. You two enjoy your lunch." Cruz patted Raiden on the shoulder as he passed while Raiden winked. They exchanged a few quiet words, but Jason missed them when his phone buzzed, and he glanced down.

River: *Do you have someone in mind for a date? If so, is it someone there or here? Don't leave me in suspense.*

By the time Jason looked back up, Cruz was

gone. Jason stood and closed the space between them. He swiped his lips across Raiden's cheek. "Come here, sexy. Smile for my soon-to-be brother-in-law." Jason moved closer and held out his phone to take a picture.

Raiden threw his hand up, laughing as Jason snapped the picture. "No. I'm still a mess."

Jason smiled as he stared down at the image. Raiden had done a good job of hiding his injuries but not his happy smile or sexy lips. With a shrug, he went ahead and sent the image to River.

Jason: *Meet Raiden. He didn't want me to take his pic, lol.*

River: *Oh my gosh, Jason! He's beautiful. You have to bring him to the wedding. I'm not taking no for an answer.*

Jason showed the message to Raiden.

"When and where is this wedding?" Raiden asked, eyeing the messages.

"In six weeks in Florida." He shoved his phone in his back pocket. "And since someone dropped ten grand I didn't want in my account, I can mysteriously afford to take us."

Raiden didn't look the least bit sorry. "Ten grand? Imagine that. That must've been one hell of a nice surprise."

A laugh stuck in Jason's throat. He swallowed it down, but he couldn't stop his smile. Raiden was just so damn stubborn. "I tell you what is one hell of a nice surprise. Seeing you. What brings you by?"

Raiden shrugged. "Since all my appointments with clients have been cancelled for the next few weeks, I was bored and took a chance that you get a lunch break."

"You're a hell of a guesser. I do get a lunch break and you're just in time." He paused for effect. "Plus, it's not at a set time. I can take my break whenever I want." The way Raiden smiled made his ridiculousness worthwhile. He hated to make Raiden's smile fall. "I only get thirty minutes, though. That's not really enough time to go anywhere."

Raiden shrugged. He honestly seemed unbothered. "That's fine. I can just spend a few minutes bugging you and then I'll let you eat."

Jason snagged the hem of Raiden's button-down shirt and lured him closer. "You have me for the full thirty. I rarely eat lunch."

A hint of annoyance flared to life in Raiden's expression. "Why? You need to eat."

With a shrug, Jason wrapped his arms around Raiden and kissed his ear. He didn't want to admit that he saved money that way. His whole life, he had been poor. He had to do what he had to do to survive. "It's fine. I'll just nibble on you instead."

"Okay," Raiden said, sounding as if he pouted. "I'll accept this today, but tomorrow, you'll start bringing your lunch. When I leave here, I'll go by the store and pick you up some things."

Jason pressed his face to Raiden's shoulder, hiding his smile and inhaling Raiden's scent. He smelled amazing. "You make me wish we could go home right now."

Raiden rubbed his back. "You should tell me about this wedding before I get sad about not being able to take you home right now. I thought you said your brother had cut you from his life."

As much as he didn't want to, Jason pulled away. "It seems I'm still family. River has kept texting me since the move, and he says Nash wants me there for the wedding. So much so, they're offering to pay for my trip, but that's not happening. What do you think? Want to spend the weekend in Florida with me in six weeks?"

"Of course." Raiden's tone was too bright to call him a liar. "I'm glad your brother hasn't given up. We should definitely be there for his big day." Jason swore he heard every word, but he couldn't look away from Raiden's sexy lips as he spoke. "We should..." Jason kissed him. "... go ahead and book..." Jason kissed him again. "... our flight." Jason kissed him deeper, cutting off the words. Raiden chuckled against his lips. "I give up."

Jason pulled away. "Okay. I'm listening. You want to go ahead and book our flight."

Raiden visibly fought a smile. He shook his head. "You're a mess. Come here." He grabbed the collar of Jason's t-shirt and pulled him in for another kiss. It seemed ridiculous to be so happy so fast, but Jason had never been this lucky. He had never felt this much hope. He wouldn't let this end. Whatever it took.

SIX

AFTER A FEW WEEKS OFF, RAIDEN EASED BACK into working. He had an elderly client who liked for Raiden to join him every other week at bingo. Charles had a lifelong partner who had passed two years earlier. Since then, Charles had hired Raiden to spend time with him. Charles was merely lonely and had worried when Cubs for Rent had called to cancel plans on his behalf. It was nice, having someone who cared. Raiden couldn't skip two bingo dates in a row. Charles didn't have anyone else. Being with Charles and hearing him tell the same hundred stories about his partner, Raiden made a decision. These would be the only clients he accepted from now on. He wouldn't risk losing Jason. He wanted a hundred boring stories to share when he got to Charles' age. That wouldn't happen if he fucked things up with Jason. There wasn't enough money in the world for Raiden to lose him.

Oddly, it was harder than Raiden expected, being away from Jason on a Saturday night. It was crazy how quickly he had become accustomed to being home with Jason every night. Thankfully, Charles never stayed out late and Raiden found himself unlocking his front door by ten. For a moment, as he stepped through the door, Raiden almost turned around and went back out, thinking he was in the wrong house. Jason standing in the middle of Raiden's transformed living room was the only thing that stopped him.

Raiden stepped inside and closed the door. His head turned from right to left, taking in the scene. The furniture had been pushed against the wall, making room for the huge tent Jason had erected in the living room. Jason only wore pajama pants and smiled like a mischievous child. Raiden was helpless against him.

"What's all this?"

Jason motioned at his work. "This is the first time you haven't been home when I am, so I took the opportunity to surprise you."

"I'm definitely surprised." Raiden kicked off his

shoes and dumped his phone and keys on the table by the door. "You still haven't told me what it is."

"Come see for yourself." Jason's excitement was hard to ignore. He looked proud. Raiden couldn't let his effort go to waste. A smile stretched his lips as he rushed across the room to get a look at his surprise. Jason stopped him before he could duck inside the tent. "First things first. Where's my kiss?"

Raiden snaked his arms around Jason's neck and shuffled close. "It's right here, baby. It's been lingering on my lips all night." He didn't realize how true his claim had been until Jason's lips touched his. Raiden chest filled with an unnamed emotion, swelling with affection and stirring something else. The weeks he had been with Jason were the happiest he had ever been in his life. Jason's kiss always added to that, taking Raiden to a level he hadn't known existed. Things turned heated. Raiden had to make himself take a step back.

"I want my surprise."

With a chuckle, Jason moved away and swept open the flap of the tent, revealing the magical world he had created inside. Raiden covered his mouth. He couldn't believe what he was seeing. Raiden had only been gone around four hours. Jason had to have been storing things some place out of sight for days.

Tiny white lights—like Christmas tree lights—covered the ceiling. They looked like twinkling stars. White fluffy blankets looked like clouds and rose petals covered the floor. In one corner, a bucket of ice, champagne, and flutes sat waiting. One wall had a huge flat image of an Arabian night. It glowed in the darkness, giving the impression they were staring at the scene from a high window. Raiden's throat swelled. It was the most romantic thing anyone had ever done for him.

He had to swallow past a growing lump to speak. "I don't know what to say. This is beautiful. I'm moved." His gaze locked on Jason. This amazing man had done this for him. "You make me wonder what I did in a past life to deserve you, because I definitely didn't earn you in this one."

Jason's serious expression made the moment seem all the more poignant. "You earn me every day by being better to me than anyone else ever has. I want to be the same for you. Every time you think about me, I want you to know in your heart that you can always count on me."

"I missed you." Even to Raiden's ears, he sounded emotional.

Jason took his hand and led him to where the champagne sat waiting. He urged Raiden to sit and poured him a glass. "Obviously, I missed you too," Jason said with a chuckle as he joined Raiden on the floor. He glanced around. "I'd love to travel around the world with you, so we could have this view for real, but this is the best I can do."

"This is better." Raiden didn't want Jason to think his effort was wasted. "No airports or jet lag. Mystery illnesses from all the germs." Raiden drained his glass, set it aside, and shifted to his knees. He crawled Jason's way. "With your version of a getaway, I don't have to worry I'm touching you too much in public, and I don't have to wait to do this." Raiden toppled Jason onto his back and straddled his hips before settling down on Jason's chest. He cuddled him as close as possible. With his ear pressed to Jason's chest, Raiden soaked in the sound of Jason's heart beating. It sounded steady and strong. Just like the man. Sometimes, Raiden thought he should be absolutely terrified of Jason. At any moment, he could crush Raiden. The thing was, Jason was too perfect to doubt. His presence was so strong in Raiden's life that Raiden felt like they had known each other forever and things would always be this way.

Jason stroked his back. "I guess that's all true. If I

had to choose, I'd rather have more time holding you than sitting on a plane."

A bark of laughter escaped Raiden. "I'm glad this rates higher than that."

Jason didn't take the bait. "I'd still love to see you on the beach, though. The sun on your skin. Your hair ruffled by the wind." Raiden closed his eyes and listened to the sound of Jason's voice. "I'd love to take your picture at night with the Eiffel Tower lit up in the background. Oh, or the castle in the Magic Kingdom."

Raiden chuckled. A smile wouldn't stop stretching his lips. "That's a bit of a jump from France to Disney."

"Not really." Jason's arms tightened around him, making Raiden feel loved and safe. "I want to do everything and go everywhere with you. That's the point I was trying to make, I guess."

"We'll get there someday," Raiden promised.

"You make it sound like we'll always be together."

Raiden went still at Jason's quietly spoken words. He didn't even breathe as he tried to decide what to say. In the end, he went with the truth. It was best to know now if Jason didn't feel the same. "That's what I want."

Jason didn't as much as hesitate. "Me too. I've never been this happy."

Air filled Raiden's lungs. Relief washed over him. When Raiden had asked Jason to move in, he had done it in the least serious way possible, in case Jason laughed. Now that Jason had been there a few weeks, Raiden acknowledged he was simply crazy. He had jumped in with both feet like a total lunatic because he was admittedly on his last straw with life. Raiden had been scratching for a lifeline, but he had found something else. He wasn't sure if it would last, but Raiden wanted this crazy and impulsive thing he had created with Jason. Raiden needed Jason to want it too.

WITH HIS HEART IN HIS THROAT, JASON STROKED Raiden's back. They hadn't talked about why he was here before tonight. Jason had been needing those words from Raiden. Every second he had been living under this roof, Jason had feared they would eventually become the roommates Raiden had initially offered. He hated the thought of moving his things down the hall and watching Raiden eventually move on to someone else. Jason needed

Raiden to acknowledge they were real, and this was going somewhere. They were in this to build a future. Now that Raiden had finally admitted it, Jason wanted to roar and beat his chest. He wished the entire world could see them and know Raiden was his. Instead, he kept caressing Raiden's skin while the pressure built in his chest.

Raiden shifted, bracing his weight on his palms beside Jason before lifting his head and kissing Jason's chest. "You're so gorgeous. Inside and out." Raiden whispered the words against Jason's bare chest. Jason felt the words more than he heard them. "I want to hold you all night, but I also want to fuck you."

Jason swallowed at the intensity in Raiden's claim. "Okay."

When Raiden's chin lifted and their gazes met, Jason had to swallow again. Raiden looked wicked and determined. "Is it? I'm not sure you completely understand me. I want to peel these pajama pants down your legs, spread those sexy cheeks, and fuck you. Can you handle that, Jason? Will you let me inside?"

This was unexpected but not unpleasantly so. While Jason preferred to be in control, he had no issues with bottoming. Jason reached beneath the table and grabbed the lube and condoms he had stashed there. He passed them Raiden's way. "You'll need these."

Triumph flashed in Raiden's eyes as he accepted Jason's offering. Without a word, he went to work. Raiden quietly undressed and then stripped Jason. Jason watched with an aching cock as Raiden rolled a condom down his length. He coated the outside with lube, stroking more than necessary and giving Jason a show.

Their gazes met and held. Raiden pushed Jason's thighs apart and scooted closer. He two-handed Jason's cock. Jason nearly jackknifed off the floor. Raiden possessed an unnatural talent for pleasing him. He fingered Jason's hole, lubing and stretching while Jason squirmed and sucked air. Raiden curled one finger inside and rubbed. Jason saw stars. His dick jumped and leaked.

"Say you're mine."

Jason froze at the demand. He held Raiden's stare. His lust-coated mind took a moment to process the demand. "I'm yours."

Raiden didn't look appeased. "Are you, Jason? I'm not playing games with you. Are you mine?"

He didn't hesitate. Jason gave him a sharp nod.

"I'm yours." His voice sounded as strong as his conviction. Jason absolutely belonged to Raiden.

"Good." Without warning, Raiden thrust inside Jason, going full to the hilt. Since he hadn't had time to tense, all Jason could do was moan as Raiden rocked, massaging him internally at the perfect angle. He should have known. Jason should have realized Raiden would be this way. Perfect. Practiced. He openly watched Jason's every reaction. Raiden found the perfect spot and didn't move. "Take what you want," Raiden said while rubbing Jason's dick. "Come on, sexy. Use me to get off."

Desperation had Jason's hips lifting. He used every bit of his muscle control to grind down on Raiden's cock. Jason lost himself to the pleasure as he moved and squirmed, using Raiden. He turned crazed. It wasn't enough. He couldn't get what he wanted from this angle. Jason pushed, taking Raiden to the floor before squatting above him and grinding downward. Raiden moaned and gasped, digging his fingers into Jason's skin and holding on as Jason used him. He took Raiden's cock, riding it hard as he sought the oblivion it offered. Raiden felt better than good. Jason liked it hard and he took it. Raiden grabbed Jason's dick and squeezed. Jason saw stars. The world exploded. With his head thrown back, Jason growled as cum shot from his cock and coated Raiden's skin. He fucked Raiden's hand as he punished his asshole with Raiden's dick. He was in another world. Jason existed in some place that only Raiden could take him. A cry sounded below him and Jason's chin dropped. He had to watch Raiden joining him. Raiden didn't disappoint. A silent cry tore from Raiden's open mouth as he strained beneath Jason. It was beautiful. They were beautiful. Jason would kill for this man. Nothing or no one would take him from Jason. This was his happiness. His. He was done with everything and everyone else. Jason's life was here now. With Raiden. Forever.

SEVEN

Over the years of working as an escort, Raiden had gotten really good at hiding his nervousness. The looming idea of meeting Jason's brother, that was something different. He was not good enough to meet anyone's family and Raiden fucking knew this. It was terrifying. He was sick with dread. Raiden one hundred percent expected Jason's brother to open the door, take one look at him, and snarl while prying Jason from Raiden's grasp.

Jason brought Raiden's hand to his lips as they climbed the stairs to an adorable house on a quiet street. "Are you okay, sexy?"

Raiden flashed him a smile that was probably more of a grimace, but Raiden couldn't help it. "I'm great." He stopped short of flashing Jason a thumbs-up, but just barely. That was how close he was to losing his shit. It wasn't that he didn't want to be here. He honestly couldn't wait to meet Jason's family, but Raiden was by no definition respectable. People did not bring him home to meet their people.

"Are you sure?"

Before Raiden could answer, the door flew open and a giant filled the entire space. Raiden was transfixed. The guy was tall, dark, big, and hairy, but his smile was sweet.

"Jason," he boomed, making Raiden flinch.

"Big brother," Jason said, walking into the guy's arms. This was Nash? That was all Raiden could think. They looked nothing alike. Nash lifted Jason off his feet with his hug. Raiden wondered if all Jason's bones popped simultaneously. The guy was massive.

Raiden pasted on a smile as Nash's gaze swung his way. "This must be Raiden."

Raiden smiled. "It's nice to meet you."

"You too." He shook Raiden's hand, engulfing it. Raiden half expected to get his hand broken, but Nash was gentle.

He went back to eyeing Jason, as if assessing his health. "Have you put on a little weight?"

Raiden couldn't miss his chance. He patted Jason's stomach. "Isn't it sexy?"

Jason blushed. It was adorable. "Raiden makes me eat." He sounded exactly like a guilty kid.

Nash's stare landed on Raiden again. "Thank you for that."

It was Raiden's turn to fight a blush. Nash sounded genuine. Thankfully, Jason saved him by taking over the conversation.

"Where's my soon-to-be brother-in-law?"

Nash moved aside, revealing a frazzled-looking tiny guy who was practically running in circles behind Nash. He glanced their way and tossed them a quick wave.

Nash flashed them a tight smile. "He's a little stressed, worrying about everyone coming over, being happy while they're here, and thinking Raiden won't like him."

"Well, that's enough of that," Raiden said, stepping past Nash. "I've got this." He was in his element when someone else was in need. There was no way in hell Raiden would let River think he didn't like him. Weddings were stressful enough. He pitched his voice to as cheerful as possible as he crossed the room. "You must be River. It's so nice to finally meet you." He caught a quick glimpse of surprise before Raiden pulled him into a hug. "Jason is always telling me about you. He's so happy that you're marrying Nash, and he doesn't have to worry about him anymore."

"Oh. That's sweet." River sounded overwhelmed. "You must be Raiden."

Raiden nodded as he held River's stare. The guy was adorable. Big blue eyes. A smatter of freckles across his nose. Raiden wanted to stare at him all day. Nash was a lucky one. "Tell me how to help. Put me to work. This is supposed to be your weekend. I don't want you stressing over everything alone. I'm here to help."

River's chest heaved. He looked ready to cry. "Honestly, I could use the help, but I don't even know where to start. Everyone is coming here tonight for a pre-wedding party. It's mostly my family, so it shouldn't be a big deal, but I want everyone to be happy and I don't know what I'm doing."

Raiden put his arm around him and squeezed. "Come on. Let's find you a drink. Sometimes, you just need a glass of wine to make everything better."

River's shoulders relaxed. "You sound just like my mom."

"Good. Then I know your mom and I will be fast friends."

"You're so tall. I didn't expect that. Do you hit your head a lot? Oh, do men follow you everywhere? You're very pretty. I feel like men probably trip over themselves to get to you. Do people ask you to reach high things for them in stores?"

Raiden laughed as he felt River relax a little more with every question he asked. He definitely felt more at peace now that he had jumped in with both feet. Jason's family would love him if it was the last thing he did. He refused to believe otherwise. Jason meant too much. He meant everything.

PRIDE SWELLED IN JASON'S CHEST AS HE watched Raiden lead River into the kitchen. He always knew how to best take care of people. Jason imagined that was why so many people paid good money to go out with him. It was hard to resist Raiden's charm.

"Damn. You did good. I've been trying to calm River all day."

Jason watched Raiden until the final wisp of his clothing disappeared before focusing on Nash. It was damn good to see his face. He hadn't realized how much he had missed Nash until now. "Raiden is pretty amazing. He'll make sure River calms down. How about you? Are you getting nervous?"

Nash closed the door and turned a luminous grin Jason's way. "Hell, no. I was ready to get married a week after we met." Nash laughed as he made the confession. "This is the life I've always wanted. In truth, the only nervousness I feel is worrying River will come to his senses before I can get him locked down."

Jason shook his head. "That's not happening. He loves you. You're really lucky." And Jason was a little jealous. By tomorrow afternoon, Nash would officially have a new family. A fresh beginning. He could walk away from Jason and never look back. In fact, despite this invitation to take part, Jason already felt left behind. Nash would join River's family and Jason would be alone in the world. He fought hard to keep smiling, but even to him, it felt faked. Tomorrow, he would lose the only family he had.

Nash eyed Jason's hands. "Where are your bags?"

"In the car."

At Jason's answer, Nash opened the door again. "I'll help you bring them in."

Jason didn't budge. "Oh. I figured we'd get a

hotel room. This is your weekend. We don't want to be in the way."

A deep line appeared between Nash's eyebrows. "You're my brother. It's not possible for you to be in the way. Plus, we only get you for the weekend. We don't want to share you with a hotel."

Before Jason could argue again, Raiden and River reappeared. They held wine glasses and wore matching smiles. River looked a hundred times better.

"Oh, are you two headed out to get the bags?" Raiden asked, surprising Jason. "I was just about to ask about that. River already showed me our room. It's adorable. I'll need to get ready soon. River says his mom always shows up early and I want to be ready to jump in to help when she gets here."

Nash chuckled. "See? Told you you're staying."

With a shrug, Jason headed out to their rental car to grab their bags. They didn't have a ton of stuff, since they were only staying two nights, but they also had several outfits since there were a million and one things happening over the weekend. Jason grabbed a bag and Nash grabbed the other. They headed back toward the house.

"Raiden seems nice. I appreciate him jumping in with River."

Jason nodded. "He's a good person." Just the thought of Raiden had Jason's smile turning genuine. "I should probably confess; we're already living together."

"Wow." Nash didn't sound judgmental. Only surprised. "You've only been gone two months and you've already turned your whole life around. It sounds like Vegas has been good to you."

"It has been." Jason's happiness re-emerged. He couldn't fault Nash for moving on. They had never really had a family they could be proud to claim. He wanted Nash to be settled and happy. "I love my new job. My check actually hits my checking account every two weeks on time. I'm living in a nice house with the perfect guy. River and you should come visit, by the way. There's a ton of fun shit to do around town. Raiden and I could take you gambling."

Nash nodded as he opened the door and led Jason back inside. "Maybe at Christmas. What do you think? We haven't had a real family Christmas together. River and I could fly in and stay a week or so. We could do the tree and everything."

The backs of Jason's eyes stung. "That sounds nice. I'll talk to Raiden about it."

Nash led him down the hall and into a large

bedroom. Everything was brightly decorated and nice. It hit Jason how different their lives were now. Nash and he had never lived in a nice place and had expensive things as children. Their clothes had come from secondhand shops and they never had anything name brand. Now they lived in gorgeous houses and had even more gorgeous men. He sat on the end of the large bed and took it all in.

The truth of their current circumstances had Jason holding Nash's stare. "We got lucky."

Nash's serious expression matched the moment of revelation. He gave Jason a sharp nod. "Yes and no. Part of it was dumb luck. The rest of it was determination. River shouldn't have looked my way, but he did. Now I'm dead set he won't regret that decision."

Jason got it. He felt his brother on every level in that moment. Raiden shouldn't have taken a chance on him, but he had. Jason would not let him regret that lapse in judgment. As if he felt Jason's need for him, Raiden appeared in the doorway. Their gazes met and held. Love washed over Jason. They had only been together a month and a half, but they had spent that entire time underneath each other's feet and sharing the same bed. They ate together, showered together, and spent hours talking. When

Jason worked, he texted nonstop and counted the seconds until he could go home. He was happy. Whole.

"I'll let you two get ready," Nash said, breaking the spell as he headed out.

Raiden smiled and stepped aside, letting Nash pass. The moment they were alone, Raiden closed the door and focused on Jason again. "They're nice. I like them."

"You're nice."

Raiden snorted at the compliment. "I'm over the top when I get nervous. Sorry about that."

"You're sexy," Jason said, not backing down.

"I'm covered in airport germs. We should take a shower."

Jason stood and headed for the bathroom inside their assigned bedroom. He peeked inside. The bathroom was nice. It had a huge walk-in shower. Big enough for two. Jason glanced over his shoulder to share the news. Raiden pressed against his back. His arms encircled Jason's waist. "You're so sexy. I can't resist touching you." Raiden kissed Jason's shoulder. "You should get undressed so I can scrub your back. I'll grab our stuff."

Jason's dick stirred as he watched Raiden move to grab their toiletries from their bag. Raiden didn't sound like it was Jason's back he planned to scrub, and Jason was onboard. He peeled off his shirt and headed for the shower, firing it to life. Jason tested the water, trying to think of anything other than Raiden's beautiful body. They were in his brother's house. He needed to have some self-control. When the air stirred behind him, Jason turned. He nearly swallowed his tongue. Raiden was nude, waiting, and hard. But it was his eyes that nearly crippled Jason. They sparkled with desire and something else. Something more. Jason wanted everything Raiden offered with that look. Raiden held his stare as he slipped past Jason and into the shower. Jason nearly stepped inside with him while still clothed. That was how captivated he was by Raiden's stare.

Raiden's laughter stopped him. "You might want to take off your pants."

Jason quickly finished stripping before overcoming Raiden. He didn't stop moving until he had Raiden backed against the shower wall. He ate at Raiden's mouth, kissing him hard and deep. Jason couldn't get enough. Not once in Jason's life had he felt this way. Before leaving this town, he hadn't been free to care about anyone. He had gone into every one-night stand knowing that was all it would ever be. His dad would destroy anyone if Jason dared to care about them. Now his dad was dead. Jason was free. Something about freely returning to this town, with Raiden and without fear, had Jason feeling twice as much for Raiden. That was a lot, considering how much he already felt before leaving Vegas. This man was his life now.

Raiden pushed at Jason's chest. When Jason took a step back, he didn't have time to question why Raiden would push him away. Raiden dropped to his knees. Jason's knees almost buckled as Raiden swallowed his cock. Raiden's eyes flipped upward. He boldly held Jason's stare as he sucked Jason's dick. Everything Raiden did was sexy as fuck. He made Jason weak. Jason stroked Raiden's jaw, feeling the way it worked as Raiden licked, sucked, and swallowed. His hips rolled without thought. He fucked Raiden's mouth while he watched Raiden pleasure him. He was like a goddamn porn star. Everything Raiden did was a show—like he relished being watched and equally loved making Jason happy. It was a powerful combination. Jason couldn't stand against Raiden's magic. There was nothing Jason wouldn't give him, tolerate, or do to keep him. Life with Raiden was a dream.

Jason had to fight to keep watching. Pleasure wanted to pull his eyes closed. Raiden sucked harder and faster as he jacked off at Jason's feet. Jason braced one hand on the wall and used the other to hold on to Raiden's hair. He took no mercy, pumping his way down Raiden's throat.

"Take it all, baby. That's good. So goddamn good. I love the way you suck me."

Jason clenched his ass cheeks, trying to hold out. He didn't want the moment to end. Raiden felt too good. He had too much talent. With one hard pull on Jason's cock, Raiden sucked Jason's orgasm from him with no permission from Jason. He bit his lip to stifle the cries that rose in his throat. Raiden didn't stop sucking. Jason's entire body shook as Raiden dragged every spasm from his body, stealing his soul. Before Jason could pull Raiden to his feet and blow his mind, Raiden turned his head and pressed his face to Jason's thigh. He cried out against his skin. The sound of him beating at his cock inside the shower only added to Jason's audio delight.

As Jason urged Raiden back to his feet and trapped him against the wall once more, he wondered if other people felt things this deeply. When their lips met and their kiss turned sweet, making Jason's eyes sting, he wondered how anyone functioned if they had someone at home who made them feel this way. It was like road rage and impatience for standing in line took on a whole new meaning. Maybe everyone was just rushing to get back to this. The realest addiction ever created. Love.

By the time guests started to arrive, Jason rode cloud nine. He was with his brother. Raiden was at his side. Life was perfect. River's parents, Charlotte and Todd, were both completely nuts. Their hilarity lightened everyone's mood while Raiden plied River with wine to keep him relaxed. At River's urging, Raiden had worn a dress and heels. He looked beautiful and happy. Jason's gaze followed him everywhere he went. Happiness owned him.

"Would you like a beer? I think I need a drink."

Jason forced his attention away from toying with Raiden's fingers to focus on his face at the question. He should be taking better care of his man. "Are you overheated with this crowd? I can fix you a drink. We could go outside."

Raiden's sexy laughter eased the tension in Jason's shoulders. "No, baby. I'm fine. I just want a drink. Let me take care of you for once. Sheesh. You don't always have to be on your toes. Visit with your friends."

A snort escaped Jason. "I know like three people here, but if you feel the need to spoil me, I won't stop you."

The way Raiden smiled had Jason ready to be alone with him already. Raiden stroked his cheek and brushed a light kiss across his lips. "Such a shameless ploy. I'll be right back."

"I'll be right here," Jason promised, even as he made Raiden work to get his hand back. He reluctantly released Raiden before Raiden stamped his foot. Still, he couldn't stop smiling as Raiden walked away.

"How have you been, Jason?"

With more than a little disappointment, Jason tore his gaze away from Raiden's ass to focus on the new arrival. Detective Craig Ranking wasn't a welcome sight, but neither did Jason hate the man. It wasn't Craig's fault that Jason's dad had been a complete piece of shit and forced the elderly detective to come around way more than necessary.

He shook Craig's hand. "I'm good. How are you?"

The detective's eyes crinkled at the corners as he

smiled. "Getting old isn't for the weak, but I'm still kicking. River tells me you've moved out to Vegas."

Jason nodded. "I took a job out that way, customizing bikes. Life is nice and quiet there."

"That has to be a nice change for you."

It really was, but Jason didn't know what Craig wanted to hear. He simply kept nodding and eyeing the crowd.

"Did Nash tell you we made an arrest in Mike's murder?"

Jason fought the urge to look Craig's way. Instead, he tried to look as if he didn't care, hoping he wouldn't show his hand. He never wanted to think about his dad again. "Why would he? Dad isn't exactly a peaceful topic for us."

Craig looked surprised by Jason's response. His eyebrows rose, and he spent a moment visibly waffling before he responded. "Because it's your mom."

A ringing started in Jason's ears. "What's my mom?"

"She confessed to his murder."

Raiden appeared at his side with a beer for Jason. "Here you go, baby."

Jason absently accepted while Raiden introduced himself to Craig. He listened with half an ear, hearing nothing but his heart beating in his ears while they chatted as if nothing happened. Jason watched as River crossed the room with Charlotte, heading their way. They both wore a luminous smile, oblivious to Jason's inner meltdown. The second they had Raiden engaged, gushing over his shoes and his long legs, Jason broke.

"Excuse me. I'll be right back." Without waiting for anyone to acknowledge him walking away, Jason headed for Nash. He snagged Nash's arm and pulled him away from the crowd. "Why didn't you tell me about Mom?"

"Oh."

Jason's eye twitched. He nearly popped a blood vessel at Nash's flippant response. "What do you mean, 'oh'? Mom gets arrested for my dad's murder and all you have to say is oh. Why didn't you call?"

Nash didn't look the least bit guilty. "What would you have done if I'd called?"

He had nothing.

"Exactly," Nash said when Jason didn't respond. "You're living in Vegas now. Let that bullshit go. I have. There isn't a thing you can do to save Mom from herself. That ship sailed a lifetime ago."

"I'll have to stay now," Jason said without thought. The fog of shock slowly lifted, and Jason couldn't abandon his mom. "There's nothing I can do from Vegas. I'll have to stay."

Nash grabbed his arm and pulled him even farther away from the crowd, ensuring their conversation stayed private. "You stop all that stupid bullshit talk right now. You're getting on that plane home Sunday, even if I have to carry you through the airport and buckle you in your seat like a kid. I won't let you ruin your life over this."

Desperation rose in Jason's throat. He felt helpless all over again. Just as he had been his entire life. "I can't turn my back on Mom."

"Why not?" Nash asked, sounding genuinely angry and bewildered. "You have no idea how much it breaks my heart to say this to you, Jason, but you need to hear it and accept it. She doesn't love us. Why would you give up Raiden, a man who does love you, to be near someone who doesn't give a damn about you? She's never getting out of prison, Jason. There's no battle to fight here."

"She's my mom," Jason said, losing his temper. "My mom is still inside her somewhere. I know it. There was a time when she was sober. A time when she made sure my clothes were clean, my lunch was packed, and gave me little notes in my lunchbox, saying she loved me. That person is still inside her and I can't walk away."

Nash's eyes fell closed. When they reopened, Nash looked wrecked. He shook his head. "I'm sorry, but no. The person you described isn't inside her. I'm the one who made sure you had clean clothes and made your lunch every day. I'm the one who slipped those notes inside your lunchbox, making you think they were from Mom, because I love you and I never wanted you to feel unwanted. I didn't want you to know what I knew. We were just one more way she kept Mike happy. She didn't kill him out of some late to the game motherly affection. She killed him because he asked for a divorce so he could marry a girl he'd been dating behind her back. A girl half his age with three small kids. I'm sorry, but she never loved us. It was never about us."

Jason wanted to scream it wasn't true, but he couldn't. He knew in his heart Nash spoke the truth. Nash didn't give him time to break down.

He squeezed Jason's shoulder. "You still have a family, and we do love you. River and I aren't going anywhere. We'll be right here, pestering you to visit us and showing up unannounced to see you, but your place is with Raiden now. He's the family you should choose, and he loves you. I can see it when he looks at you, and that's everything I've ever wanted for you. How can you even think of losing him for Mom? Look at him."

Jason turned his head. Raiden had taken off his heels. He held River's hand while River tried them on. River immediately fell over. Raiden scrambled to catch him. Loud laughter filled the room. Raiden looked his way, smiling.

Nash squeezed his shoulder again. "Are you really thinking of staying here and going back to life without him?"

Jason could barely breathe at the thought.

River waved and yelled across the room. "Look, baby. I'm tall."

He fell over again.

Raiden's eyes danced with laughter as he held River upright.

A snort escaped Jason. "No. I can't let him go." He really couldn't. Not even for his mom.

Nash gave his shoulder a pat. "Let's go join them before River breaks an ankle and we have to get married in a hospital room."

Jason nodded. "Agreed." He had already left Raiden for longer than he ever wanted. Nash was right. There was nothing for him here.

RAIDEN TRIED TO MAKE THE BEST OF JASON angrily walking away from him. Something about being here ate at Jason. His mood swung wildly from one minute to the next. One second, he would look at Raiden like Raiden hung the moon. The next, he would eye the room like life had slipped away from him. Raiden's head was a mess. His heart was silently breaking. Something about this town was choking Jason.

While holding River upright in his heels, Raiden finally broke. He couldn't fake smiling for another second. "What's that all about?" Raiden asked, nodding toward where Nash and Jason were speaking in whispers in the corner.

Craig cleared his throat. He looked guilty. "That might be my fault. I hadn't realized Nash never told Jason about their mom."

River groaned. "Yeah. Sorry. I didn't warn you not to say anything. We decided not to tell him. We worried he would drop everything and come home. He's so much better off in Vegas."

Raiden glanced between them. "What are you talking about?"

River made a dismissive motion. "Well, you

know how Jason's dad was murdered about three months ago?" He hadn't known, but he also didn't interrupt. "Anyhow, they arrested Nash and Jason's mom last week. Apparently, she confessed to everything."

"Shit." Raiden didn't know what else to say. That wasn't good. Jason hadn't said a word about any of this. He didn't talk about his family at all beyond telling stories about Nash.

Charlotte nodded. "It's so hard to let go of a toxic family, but we're here for them." She snagged River's waist and towed him against her side, relieving Raiden of his duties. "You had no idea you were so lucky growing up, did you, bub?"

"Of course, I did," River said, rolling his eyes.

Charlotte focused on Raiden with laughter in her eyes. "What about you, Raiden? What are your parents like?"

A lump immediately formed in Raiden's throat. "They were amazing. The best parents ever."

Her smile fell. Raiden wished he had lied and pretended they were still alive. "Oh, no. They've passed?"

Raiden nodded. "It's okay. Let's not make this night sad. You're getting married." He took River's hands. "How excited are you? You're going to be such a gorgeous groom. What are you wearing?" He listened with half an ear as River described his outfit and the decorations as Jason returned to his side. Raiden made small talk with his heart in his throat. Jason's eyes looked dead.

Raiden made it until he had his shoes back and everyone wandered off, leaving them alone. "You want to stay." It wasn't a question. Raiden could see it in Jason's eyes. He was done with Raiden. He needed his brother.

Jason's gaze shot to Raiden. He looked genuinely surprised. "No. Obviously, I miss my brother, but—if I stayed—I'd miss you more." He wrapped an arm around Raiden's waist and towed him closer. "In case you haven't noticed, you're under my skin, Raiden Li."

Raiden fought the happiness surging to life inside him. He needed to be realistic about this. "Even though I date other men for a living?"

"What does that have to do with anything?" Jason looked genuinely confused by Raiden's question. "I know you, baby. I see the real you." He visibly swallowed. His gaze dropped to Raiden's lips before his gaze returned to Raiden's eyes. He licked his lips, looking nervous. "In fact, I'm very much in love with everything about you. So, no, I won't leave you for this place. You're not getting rid of me that easily."

"You love me?" Even to Raiden's ears, he sounded dumbfounded. He'd never expected anyone to love him.

Jason chuckled. "Why do you sound like that? You can't be that surprised. If you haven't noticed, I pretty much live for you now. I don't want to be anywhere but where you are."

Jason's confession filled Raiden's chest. He felt like he could take over the world. "I love you too."

Jason's features shifted—like he couldn't settle on a reaction or was scared to hope. "You don't have to say it back if you don't mean it. I just need you to know how I feel. I need you to know you can't lose me."

Consternation had Raiden's eyebrows crawling toward his hairline. "Do you really think I'm the kind of person who would tell anyone I love them if I don't?"

Jason seemed to truly consider the question. Finally, he shook his head. "You don't sugarcoat things."

Raiden gave him a sharp nod. "Well, there you go. I'm in love with you, Jason Hayes. I'm glad you don't want to stay. Losing you would break my heart. I really want to go make out now."

The bright and sexy smile stretching Jason's lips made the confessions worthwhile. Maybe neither of them were strictly conventional, and no one believed they would make it but them, but Raiden now believed. Jason had said he loved Raiden. He wasn't getting away now. Whatever it took. Raiden would keep this man he hadn't expected. He wasn't dumb enough to let him get away.

EIGHT

"Blow."

Raiden leaned closer to Antonio and blew on the dice he held.

Antonio smiled like Raiden blessed him. "I'll win for sure this time."

Raiden winked. "Damn right, you will."

Antonio rolled.

"Seven. Better wins."

Raiden jumped up and down, clapping happily. It was all a ruse, of course. Antonio owned Lombardi High-Roller Casino. He always won. Still, it was a little fun to see someone win at games rigged for the house. Antonio was also one of Raiden's favorite dates. Like Raiden, Antonio's entire family was gone with the exception of distant relatives he had never met. He hired Raiden twice a year. Once for his birthday and on Thanksgiving. The two days he couldn't stand to be alone. Raiden had been more grateful for that time than Antonio knew. Maybe one day, when he no longer did this job, he would still spend those two days with him. No one should always be alone.

The crazy thing about Antonio was he was young, handsome, and loaded. He could have anyone. For reasons all his own, he chose to stay single. It was possible he was a lecherous rake whenever Raiden wasn't around. With Raiden, he was always a true gentleman. He acted like he was eighty and Raiden was the grandson he loved to dote upon. In truth, he was forty-five and not the least bit of a grandfather figure. Still, he was one of the few customers Raiden had kept since he started seeing Jason six months ago. Antonio was safe. He would never threaten Raiden's relationship.

Antonio slid his winnings Raiden's way. "For you. Call it a bonus for always being my lucky charm."

Raiden shook his head. "I couldn't. You're already too generous." He really was. Antonio paid him three times what anyone else did and refused to be told no on the matter.

It seemed he didn't like being denied now either. His light blue eyes flashed dangerously. "Take the chips, Raiden. This isn't up for debate." He leaned closer and presented his cheek to Raiden. "Kiss me and tell me who's your favorite friend."

Raiden chuckled. "You're such a bossy britches. You know you're my favorite." He pressed his lips to Antonio's cheek.

He felt Antonio smile. "Ahhh, but I do love to hear you say it."

Raiden barely leaned away and still held Antonio's arm. Yet he found himself flying backward. It took his brain a second to catch up to reality so he could recognize he had been yanked away from Antonio. Cruz now stood between Antonio and Raiden—chest heaving, and eyes flashing with fury as they latched on to Antonio. Raiden's heart jumped into his throat.

"How fucking dare you touch him? I'll kill you."

Raiden scrambled to get between them. Antonio looked deadly. Horror owned Raiden. He couldn't let this happen. Jason and Raiden never talked about what other people knew or didn't know about his job. It seemed Cruz didn't know.

"No, Cruz. You don't understand..." The words died on his lips as Cruz reared back to swing.

Without thought, Raiden lunged and placed himself bodily in front of Antonio. Everything happened at hyper speed, yet Raiden swore he saw it all in slow motion. Cruz's eyes widened, but he was too far in to stop. He pulled his punch a hair, obviously trying to stop his forward momentum, but it was too late. Raiden's head snapped back as Cruz's fist collided with Raiden's cheek. He stumbled. Antonio was there to catch him. "He's my client," Raiden said because the words were already halfway out before he had gotten punched in the face. He could no more stop his speech than Cruz could've stopped his punch.

"What?"

"I'm working," Raiden said, holding his face.

Security jumped Cruz. It was crazy how many things happened at the same time in the heat of the moment. Cruz's expression went through a thousand transitions.

Antonio held Raiden against his chest while barking orders. "You get Raiden an ice pack and find a physician. You, clear a path to my office." He focused on Cruz. "If I ever see your face in my casino again, no one will ever find you. Get him out of here." Antonio swept Raiden from his feet and headed for the back with security clearing the way.

"I can walk. It's fine."

Angry blue eyes flashed his way. "It is not fine," Antonio spat. His Italian accent thickened in his anger. "You were injured while protecting me. I cannot have that." Each word Antonio spoke was through clenched teeth.

Raiden settled in and let him have his way. He was too upset to argue too much. Cruz thought Raiden was a cheat. That much was painfully obvious. The aches in Raiden's chest were crippling. Would Cruz run straight to Jason and try to destroy them? How hard would it be? Even if Jason calmly explained this was Raiden's job, Cruz would likely look at Jason differently. It would only be a matter of time before the constant judgment of others wore him down. Then jealousy would set in. The fighting would begin. Raiden could see the end of them in the distance. One way or the other, this night would destroy them if Raiden didn't find a way to change the future. A deep sadness settled into Raiden's chest.

Antonio gently set Raiden on a leather couch in his office. Someone handed him an ice pack. Raiden held it to his cheek. His gaze landed on Antonio while Antonio paced like an angry lion.

"I'm sorry, sweetie." Honestly, Raiden didn't

know why he apologized. Somehow, this was his fault. Everything usually was. "That was my boyfriend's boss. He obviously misread the situation. I'm so embarrassed."

Antonio stopped pacing and dropped to his haunches in front of Raiden. He peeled the ice pack away from Raiden's face and eyed his injury. "Don't ever apologize to me again. Some men are just violent and that has nothing to do with you." He urged the ice pack back to Raiden's face and met his stare. "You have a very kind soul. You remind me very much of someone I used to know. Life was very cruel to him as well. My assistant will cash in your chips and deposit the money in your account. You will be well compensated for protecting me."

Irritation had Raiden dropping the ice pack to his lap and staring Antonio down, determined to stand his ground. "None of this would've happened if not for me. You don't owe me anything. Despite my position, I think of you as a friend. I wouldn't let anyone hurt you." With a huff that sounded tired even to his ears, Raiden gingerly touched the ice pack to his cheek again. "I'm also getting unfortunately accustomed to getting punched in the face. Apparently, that's this year's theme."

Antonio's features hardened. "Someone else hit you?"

Raiden nodded. "It's a long story. Basically, I accepted a new client, and he obviously expected more. When I resisted, he put me down for a few weeks. It's okay. I got a restraining order."

Antonio looked thoughtful and taken aback. "Which client is this? I didn't think you had any clients who would do such a thing."

With adrenaline pumping through his veins and pain pulsing in his cheek, Raiden wasn't thinking clearly. He spoke without considering his words. "James Renault."

Antonio physically drew back and blinked. "The boxer. You got hit by a heavyweight boxer?"

Raiden snorted. "A few times, unfortunately." Raiden tried for a smile. "I'm good. We can't let this ruin your birthday."

Antonio shook his head. "You're going home to rest. My birthday is just another day and you're hurt. We've already had a lovely dinner and I adore the pocket watch you gave me. This is a good time to hug and call it a night."

Raiden felt like shit. He had a knack for ruining things. Raiden imagined he had lost Antonio as a client. Cruz would likely ensure Raiden lost Jason.

Still, he would show as much class as possible in an impossible situation. He leaned forward and hugged Antonio. Impulsively, he pressed a quick kiss to his cheek. "Thank you for taking care of me. Despite everything, I hope you had a great birthday."

Antonio squeezed him a little tighter than usual. "Let me call a car or Jason to take you home. You shouldn't drive."

As he pulled away, Raiden flashed him a smile. "I promise I'm fine."

Even though he didn't look happy about it, Antonio nodded and helped Raiden to his feet. He held on to Raiden's hand a second longer than necessary. Before Raiden could pull away, Antonio brought Raiden's hand to his lips and pressed a kiss to the back before releasing him. "Be careful going home."

Raiden nodded. "I will." Without looking back, Raiden headed for the door. Antonio's assistant waited outside, coughing and red-faced. He looked like shit—like he had a fever and needed to go home. Raiden flashed the man a sympathetic smile as he passed. He cringed as he heard Antonio ask the man to find James Renault's number. Fuck. He should have stayed quiet. Raiden let it go. He already had too much to stress about—like the likelihood of Jason being gone by the time Raiden got home. He almost made it to his car when Cruz appeared from nowhere.

"Oh my god, Raiden. I'm so, so sorry."

Raiden barely spared him a glance as he unlocked his car. "Don't worry over it."

Cruz snatched the keys from his hand before Raiden could climb behind the wheel. "I'll drive you home. You shouldn't be driving, and I should explain to Jason in person. I feel awful. I'm a goddamn idiot. I just saw the two of you together and thought…" He didn't have to finish his thoughts. Raiden knew. Cruz shook his head, as if shaking off his reasons. "Do you want to hit me back?" He squared his shoulders as if truly readying himself for Raiden's punch.

With a sigh, Raiden shook his head. He was too endearing. Plus, it wasn't Cruz's fault. Not really. "I don't hit people."

Cruz's shoulders fell. "Well, now I'm an even bigger ass."

"Let's go," Raiden said, sounding defeated even to his ears. The last thing he wanted was to stand there all night with an ice pack pressed to his face. Raiden just wanted to go home, but Cruz had his keys. He didn't feel like fighting and he worried he might cry if he stood there too long. At least, if Cruz went home with him now, maybe he could brunt some of the damage with Jason. With his head down, Raiden stared at his feet as he circled the car and climbed into the passenger seat. There was no time like the present to get this over. Let the heartache begin.

———

THERE HAD NEVER BEEN A TIME IN JASON'S LIFE when he could kick back and play video games all night. He hadn't gotten to be a kid. Life with Raiden was the polar opposite of everything his life had been before six months ago. Before meeting Raiden a half a year earlier, Jason never even felt like a person. Now, he had his feet up. It was Saturday night, and he hadn't done shit all day. He had a game controller between his hands, a bowl of popcorn at his hip, and one eye on the clock because he was so damn ready for Raiden to get home.

When he heard the beep of the digital lock on the front door, Jason quickly switched off his game, set his popcorn on the table, and came to his feet. He always tried to meet Raiden at the door—like a happy dog. After all, he was the most ecstatic of boys. When the door flew open, angry voices reached him before he reached Raiden. Jason froze in his tracks at the sight meeting him. Cruz carried a spitting mad Raiden across the threshold.

"I'm completely capable of walking. It's not like this is the first time someone's punched me in my face."

Punched him? Jason crossed the room. Raiden held an ice pack to his cheek. Jason saw red. "What in the hell happened?" And why hadn't anyone called him?

"It was an accident," Raiden said.

"I'm so fucking sorry," Cruz said at the same time, trying to speak over the top of Raiden.

Jason plucked Raiden from Cruz's arms. Nobody carried Raiden but him. "What happened, baby?"

"It was a misunderstanding." Raiden looked and sounded on the verge of tears. "Cruz saw me at the casino and didn't know I was working. He went after Antonio and I stepped between them."

Cruz followed them, flapping his arms like he didn't know how to help but needed to do something. "He didn't look like a client of any kind to me. The guy was eyeing Raiden like his next meal and Raiden kissed his cheek."

Raiden fought to jump from Jason's arms—like he

might fight Cruz. "Like you would a family member. Goddamn, Cruz. Not every act of affection is sexual. Antonio has been a client for years. He's my friend."

Jason fought to catch up. He sat on the couch while keeping a tight hold on Raiden. "Okay. Everybody needs to take a breath and tell me what the hell is going on."

No one listened.

Cruz was back in with both feet. "Well, goddamn, Raiden. What sort of clients do you have that take you gambling and treat you like you're on a date?"

Jason's eyebrows snapped together. Cruz was already skating on thin ice. First, he had put his hands on Raiden and now he was yelling at him about his job. "A date treats him like a date," Jason said, sounding pissed off even to his ears. "Raiden is an escort. I knew exactly where he was tonight and who he was with. Why would you get involved at all?"

Cruz fell silent. He went completely still. For a moment, he became a statue before finally blinking. His gaze locked on Raiden. "You're an escort?"

Jason ignored Cruz to focus on Raiden. He checked beneath the ice pack. It wasn't too bad. "Oh, my baby. I'm so sorry. What do you want me to do? Do you want me to kill him?"

A small smile flashed across Raiden's lips. His eyes danced with laughter. The air lightened. "I don't think that's necessary. It's really okay. He barely grazed me."

"You let your boyfriend work as an escort?"

A growl reverberated off the walls of Jason's mind. Cruz really wasn't letting this go. "I don't let him do anything. Raiden is a person, and he's free to do what makes him happy. I didn't fall in love with who I thought I could make him into. I love him for him."

Raiden sniffed.

Jason's gaze shot back to his.

Raiden visibly blinked back tears. "I love you." His voice shook, breaking Jason's heart.

"Come work for me," Cruz said, cutting into their conversation. "I need someone to work the front counter and you won't have to worry about getting unwanted attention or getting hit."

Jason snapped. "He wouldn't have gotten hit if you hadn't hit him. You've got a lot of fucking nerve—"

"Okay."

Jason focused on Raiden again at the agreement.

He couldn't let Raiden get shamed into this. "No, baby. I don't want this. I don't want you to feel bullied into a job you don't want. There's nothing wrong with you. I love you just as you are."

Raiden visibly fought for air before a tear slipped from the corner of his eye. The sight shattered his heart. When Raiden finally managed to speak, he didn't say any of the words Jason expected. Instead, he ripped out Jason's heart with a microscopic view inside his mind. "I was a soul-wrecked mess when I met you," Raiden said, taking a sledgehammer to Jason's sanity, but Raiden wasn't finished. "Not only did I not want to get out of bed anymore, every day it got a little harder to lift my head. After we met, and I went back to work, I stopped accepting any clients beyond the older men who just liked to have a bridge partner or to sit and talk." A sad smile touched his lips. "I've become quite the mess. Every one of my current clients knows your name and our story. They ask about your health and happiness. But I get that other people will never see me as anything more than a whore and I don't want that for you."

"I'm sorry, Raiden."

Jason flashed an angry look Cruz's way at the interruption. "You be quiet. You've done enough."

Raiden touched Jason's cheek, bringing Jason's

attention back to him. "It's not his fault. As long as I stay in this job, no one will ever think I deserve you."

"Damn it, Raiden. I'm really, really sorry."

Jason couldn't take it anymore. Cruz had obviously made Raiden question his whole life with that hit, and Jason couldn't handle it. He had no fucks left to give about keeping his job. Nothing mattered but Raiden and Cruz had fucking hit him. "Goddamn, Cruz. Just leave already. Maybe by Monday I'll be over this, but right now, I don't even want to look at you. Get out."

Cruz swiped his hand over his eyes. His shoulders fell. "Yeah. Okay. Call me if you need anything." While looking like a defeated kid, Cruz let himself out.

Jason didn't focus on Raiden again until they were alone. "Come here." Jason shifted positions, moving until they were stretched out and cuddled together on the couch with Raiden held tightly against Jason's chest. Jason touched his lips to the shell of Raiden's ear. "Now, tell me why you don't trust me."

Raiden drew back, looking horrified. "It's not that at all."

Jason couldn't doubt him. "Okay, then tell me

what's happening inside your head that's convincing you I could possibly leave you."

Even though Raiden hesitated, he didn't make Jason beg for the truth. "Life has already ripped everyone from me in an instant. I know it could happen again. I know I don't have the power to stop it from happening, but I can control this. If my job is something that could take you away from me, I have to fix it."

Even though Jason knew there was nothing he could say that would take away Raiden's fear, he had to try. That was his job. "Baby, fixing it implies there's something broken. You know how you said you're no longer taking clients that could harm us, I already knew that, because I trust you. I never made you swear you wouldn't accept a high-paying job for sex, because I knew you wouldn't do that to me." Jason kissed the tip of Raiden's nose. "This is real, and it's strong. I'd go as far as to say our relationship is stronger than people who've been together for years, because we both understand all too well how cold life is alone. We know how lucky we are. It's really important to me that you don't change who you are because you think it's what I want. Hear me. I love you, Raiden Li. I cannot be convinced to stop. Please don't do something that'll make you miserable to try to please me. I'm already the happiest man alive. You couldn't make me happier unless you married me and kept me forever. Like, for real, I'm in this life with you for good. Let's get ready for bed."

Rather than immediately agreeing, Raiden's mouth lifted in one corner in a sardonic smile. "Cruz is probably still sitting on the porch. He drove me home in my car."

Jason drew a slow breath in through his nose and massaged the spot between his eyes. "Okay. You get your sexy ass in bed and I'll deal with Cruz."

With a nod, Raiden leaned in and pressed his lips to Jason's before rolling to his feet. "I'll be waiting."

Jason watched Raiden as he headed for their bedroom until he couldn't see a single hint of him before he stood. With a sigh, he went in search of Cruz. Jason found him exactly where Raiden guessed—sitting on the porch steps. Jason dropped down beside him.

Cruz glanced his way. "Have you come to drop kick me from your life?"

Jason was tempted, but he also recognized that Cruz didn't know him. Not really. He didn't know anything about Jason's past or what drove him. "Not yet, no." They sat in silence, side by side, staring into the darkness while Jason tried to decide how to handle this. "My father was a sadistic bastard," Jason said from nowhere and with no plan. The confession just popped out. He rolled with it. After all, it was too late to stop now. "He beat all his kids and his wife, but worse than that, he got off on hurting us mentally. It was so subtle and cruel that I didn't even recognize some of it until I was grown." Cruz turned his way and gave Jason his full attention, so Jason kept talking. "I remember this one time; my mom was dressed for the Florida heat. Short shorts and low-cut tank top. He screamed and ranted about how she was showing off the body that belonged to him, purposely tempting other men. She went inside and changed clothes and I never saw her wear shorts above the knee again. Then, one day—out of the blue —he started taunting her, calling her old and frumpy. He said she never dressed sexy anymore, and he was tired of being with someone who couldn't be bothered to tempt him." Jason shook his head and kept staring at the night sky. He would never, ever forget the ever present and deep unhappiness in his mom's eyes. "No matter what he said or how he contradicted himself, she would change to suit his game." Jason finally focused on Cruz. "I'm not my dad. Raiden won't be coming to work for you to suit the picture you have in your mind of what he should be like. I love him exactly as he is."

"It's not about what Raiden does," Cruz said, obviously still determined to argue. "I'm not passing judgment on him. The escort business is dangerous. I don't want him to get hurt. It's already happened twice."

Jason growled in his frustration. "Yeah, and one of those times was by you."

Cruz scrubbed at his face. "I know. I said I was sorry."

"I know you thought you were sticking up for me," Jason said, offering an olive branch. "You have no idea how much I appreciate you. You gave me a job and a place to live. A second chance at life. Without your help, I probably would've ended up in prison, or like my father—dead. But I don't need your help with this. Okay?"

Cruz nodded. "Yeah. Okay. If Raiden changes his mind, though, I'll keep a place open for him."

Jason nodded and stood. "Come on. There's a spare bedroom with your name on it."

Cruz waved off his offer. "Nah. I'll call a cab to take me back to the casino. I don't want my bike sitting in that parking lot all night. Thanks for the offer, though. Tell Raiden I'm sorry again."

A snort escaped Jason. "I'm pretty sure he's heard it enough."

A grunt of laughter escaped Cruz. "All right. It's possible I have a bit of a guilty conscience. It's pretty common for me to lose my temper and wreck everything."

A smile tugged at the corners of Jason's mouth. "None of us are perfect. Raiden and I both know you wouldn't hit him on purpose. Not that I'm over it," Jason tacked on, because Cruz had hit Raiden and that was unacceptable.

Cruz stood. "Fair enough. I'll let you get back to him."

Jason patted Cruz's shoulder and headed back inside. He still needed to set Raiden at ease. Jason hadn't known Raiden had been struggling with fear of Jason leaving him. Raiden hadn't let on. Jason needed to fix this. Nothing mattered as much as Raiden and their relationship. Raiden would damn well know his importance. Jason couldn't have things any other way. Otherwise, he didn't deserve the love Raiden had risked on him.

RAIDEN WAS HALFWAY THROUGH BRUSHING HIS

teeth before everything Jason said penetrated his thick skull. For a moment, he stared at himself in the mirror with his toothbrush hanging out of his mouth.

"Wait."

He spit his toothpaste in the sink and rushed from the bathroom. Jason was already curled up between the sheets.

"Did you ask me to marry you a few minutes ago?"

A sexy rumble of laughter filled the air. "It took you long enough. Yes. I thought that was where we were headed, or at least I hoped." Even once Jason confirmed his thoughts, Raiden still couldn't take it in. Thankfully, Jason kept talking, saving him from picking a reaction. "I would love to have your last name. Imagine me introducing myself as Jason Li. Everyone would want to know the story of how I ended up with the last name Li, and then I'd get to brag about how the sexiest man in the world gave it to me." Jason's smile said he meant every word. He looked exactly like he pictured himself having that conversation with people.

"You want to take my last name."

Even though it hadn't been a question, Jason still treated it as one. His expression softened. "Well, yeah. You had a great family, so I could never ask you to give up that final piece of them. I had a horrible family and would love to ditch every reminder. Plus, I love you. I want all of you. Even your name."

Raiden's feet moved in the direction of his heart. He crawled on the bed and stripped the blankets from Jason's nude body until he could straddle him. Raiden stared down at the man between his thighs. Love swelled in his chest. "I've always heard bad boys make the best husbands."

Jason's hands skimmed up Raiden's thighs, slipping beneath Raiden's robe. "I suppose that's true, since I would never let you down."

A smile snapped to Raiden's lips. "I meant me." His smile melted away, replaced with a solemn air befitting the moment. "I'll be the best husband."

Jason twisted the tie of Raiden's robe around his hand and tugged, pulling it loose. The two halves of his robe fell apart, revealing his nudity. While holding Raiden's stare, Jason pushed the material down Raiden's shoulders while holding his stare. Halfway down his arms, Jason's hold tightened on the robe. He tugged, using the material to tow Raiden in for a kiss. Raiden's eyes fell closed as their lips met. The air stuttered from his lungs. Jason always moved him. Raiden hadn't known it was possible to love someone so much until Jason barged into his life.

As their tongues stroked, Jason's erection poked him. Raiden smiled against Jason's lips and lifted. He shifted positions, trapping Jason's cock between their bodies. Raiden rocked. His dick stirred to life with Jason's erection massaging him. They were always so hot for each other. Raiden hoped that never died. Right now, though, he wanted to make love to Jason. Raiden needed to seal their promise to marry with sweet passion. Jason moaned. The sound vibrated through their kiss as Raiden kept up a steady pace. He used the friction between their bodies to pleasure Jason. Raiden's hips thrusted. Their kiss turned hotter. Jason's fingers dug into Raiden's skin as he tried controlling Raiden's pace. Raiden fought the urge to reach between them and help things along. That wasn't what he wanted. Raiden wanted to come with only the sensation of Jason's dick rubbing his. He slowed, purposefully teasing them both. The torment was so sweet.

Jason tore his mouth away and growled. "Goddamn it, Raiden. Fuck me."

A chuckle that sounded evil even to Raiden's ears slipped past his lips. "No. You'll come for me like this. You can do it, Jason."

Jason tilted his chin up. He squeezed his eyes shut and sucked air, visibly straining toward release.

Raiden kept thrusting. "That's it, gorgeous. I'm on your dick. Rubbing. Teasing. Getting you off. Give me that cum."

Jason's entire body stiffened.

Raiden held his breath.

Hot cum filled the space between them as a loud gasp ripped from Jason. Raiden couldn't look away as Jason shook between his thighs. He was a beautiful sight in the throes of passion. Jason was always flawless.

"I can't wait to tell everyone you're my husband."

Jason's eyes opened. His intensity stole Raiden's breath. In a flash, Raiden found himself trapped beneath Jason's large frame. He kissed the place on Raiden's cheek that would most likely bruise tomorrow. When he spoke against Raiden's skin, his words didn't match the sweet gesture. "I hope you're ready for a long night. I'm about to brand my name on this body."

"Good."

That was the last coherent word to pass from Raiden's lips. Jason always told the truth and made him proud. Tonight was no different.

NINE

After the tenth time of checking on Raiden, ensuring he still slept peacefully, Jason forced himself to make coffee instead of hovering. Raiden never slept this late. He hoped Raiden wasn't getting sick. If he wasn't, then Jason had to accept that Raiden had been mentally exhausted for so long, he had finally hit a wall. Jason would keep the house quiet and let him sleep. He hoped whichever issue had him sleeping the day away that sleep fixed him.

Just when Jason got comfortable in the recliner with a thick blanket covering him, Raiden wandered into the living room. His hair stood on end and there were dark circles under his eyes, matching the bruise on his cheek. Jason took one look at him and lifted the edge of the blanket. Raiden padded across the room, climbed into his lap, and settled down on Jason's chest. Jason fixed the blanket. With his lips pressed to Raiden's head, Jason closed his eyes. It didn't seem Raiden was ready to be awake yet and Jason had no problem with taking a nap. He had the love of his life in his arms and nowhere to be. It felt like the perfect day to him. It seemed the moment he dozed off, someone rang the doorbell.

"For fuck's sake," Raiden grumbled against his chest. "Can't we just have a day?"

Jason kissed Raiden's forehead. He felt a little warm. "I'll get it. You stay here and rest." He slipped from beneath Raiden, leaving him tucked in beneath the blanket. Jason tried not to worry as he headed for the door. He didn't like the thought of Raiden being sick. Without bothering to check the peephole, Jason pulled open the door. Tucker stood on the other side.

He blinked at the sight of Jason. "Hey."

"Hey." Jason returned the greeting with the same level of confused enthusiasm. Tucker was a pleasant surprise when Jason had half expected to find Cruz still on their doorstep.

Tucker visibly shook off his shock over seeing Jason still there. "Is Raiden home?"

Jason stepped back and waved Tucker inside. "Come on in. Raiden's a little under the weather today, but he's home."

With a nod, Tucker stepped inside. "I won't stay long. I just have some news I wanted to deliver in person."

Jason closed the door behind him and turned. Raiden magically had two blankets now—like he had gotten cold without Jason's body heat to warm him.

Raiden peeked out from his cocoon. "Hey, Tucker. Sorry. I'd offer you some coffee or something, but I'm not feeling great today."

Tucker froze halfway to the couch and eyed Raiden. "Why do you still have bruises?"

Raiden struggled to sit up and Jason rushed to help. He flashed Jason a grateful smile before focusing on Tucker again. "I'm a scrapper who can't scrap," he answered with heavy laughter in his voice. "I jumped in the middle of a fight at a casino, trying to break it up, and got hit."

While Raiden spoke, Jason felt his forehead and cheeks. He wasn't burning up, but he felt warmer than he should. Jason focused on Tucker. "Would you like something to drink? I'm going to grab Raiden some water and Tylenol."

Tucker shook his head. "No, thank you. I'm not staying long. Orion, my husband, is getting us settled into a hotel. We decided to take advantage of this delivery to slip in a vacation."

With a nod, Jason headed for the kitchen. He kept one ear on the conversation in the living room as he grabbed a bottle of water from the fridge and some pills from the cabinet.

"Are you okay?"

Jason strained to hear Raiden's response. He hadn't had time to ask Raiden that himself today. "Yeah. My client's assistant was coughing and red in the face last night. I'm thinking he passed along whatever he has to me. Unfortunately," he tacked on, sounding tired. "What brings you by?"

Jason made his way back to the living room in enough time to hear Tucker's answer.

Tucker's gaze moved between them as Jason helped Raiden take his pills. "We had an unexpected late-night call from James last night. He asked to settle things quickly and quietly. I was prepared to haggle and drag out his suffering, but his offer was too good for me to balk. He transferred the money right away. So, as promised." He passed a check Raiden's way.

Raiden stared at it in silence before passing it Jason's way.

Jason blinked at the number of zeros. He had never seen a check so big, which didn't take much. In truth, he hadn't seen much of anything in his life. He set the check on the end table before focusing on Tucker. "Is this for real?"

Tucker chuckled. "Yeah. It surprised us too. I guess his career and reputation are worth quite a bit to him. Anyhow, I wanted to deliver the news in person. Plus, this makes my trip a tax write-off," he added with a boyish grin.

"I'm glad you're here. For more than just the check," Raiden added. His voice had turned somewhat scratchy. Raiden cleared his throat. "This saves me a phone call. I've decided to mark myself as unavailable for new clients."

Jason's gaze sharpened. He thought they had settled this.

Raiden wasn't finished. "This check definitely makes the decision easier, but Jason and I are getting married, and I think I'd like to try my hand at being lazy for a while. A stay-at-home wife, if you will."

A smile exploded across Jason's face not only at Raiden's choice of words, but at the picture he painted. It was ridiculous how happy the idea of Raiden doing nothing made him. Raiden deserved to be free of every responsibility for a while. Plus, Jason loved the thought of them having their weekends back, doing nothing but being together.

Tucker's smile matched Jason's in happiness level. "Congrats. I'm thrilled to hear you two are getting married. What a romantic story you'll have to tell, marrying the man who saved you."

Jason almost corrected Tucker and admitted Raiden had been the one who saved him. Raiden's response had the words dying on his tongue.

"He really is my hero." Jason focused on Raiden. His gaze was locked on Jason. Love sparkled in his eyes for everyone to see. "He's also my best friend and I can't wait to be his husband." A lump formed in Jason's throat. He felt the same.

"I'll get out of y'all's hair," Tucker said, pulling their attention back his way. "Congrats again." He shook Jason's hand and nodded Raiden's way. "I hope you get to feeling better. Let me know if you need anything."

Raiden looked and sounded a little worse by the minute. "Jason is here. I have everything I need."

Tucker's gaze moved between them. "I see that.

It was good seeing you both again." With a few more pleasantries exchanged, Jason walked Tucker to the door and showed him out. He locked the door before making his way back to Raiden. Raiden already looked half asleep again.

Jason scooped him from the couch, blankets and all. "Come on, sickly angel. It's back to bed for you."

"But you're so much more comfortable than the bed." Raiden sounded like a little kid. Despite Raiden's obvious illness, Jason couldn't stop smiling.

"I'm coming with you."

Raiden snuggled closer to his chest. "Oh. That's okay, then." He nuzzled Jason's neck. "As long as I have you, I'll be fine. I love you."

"I love you too, baby," Jason said as he crawled onto the bed they shared. "I'll make you better." He would too. While Jason couldn't wait until they were legally bound, he didn't need that piece of paper to force him to keep the vows that already lived in his heart. In sickness and in health, he would always he right here, loving the man who had saved him. For as long as they both lived, and likely beyond.

KEEP AN EYE OUT FOR THE NEXT BOOK IN MESSY Hearts, *Gut-Checked.*

Please consider clicking this link and leaving a review, https://www.amazon.com/review/create-review?asin= B0835QVGQL. Reviews really help with a book's visibility, which ensures I can continue writing. Thank you, Charity.

ABOUT THE AUTHOR

Charity Parkerson is an award winning and multi-published author with several companies. Born with no filter from her brain to her mouth, she decided to take this odd quirk and insert it in her characters.

*Eight-time Readers' Favorite Award Winner
  *2015 Passionate Plume Award Finalist
  *2013 Reviewers' Choice Award Winner
  *2012 ARRA Finalist for Favorite Paranormal Romance
  *Five-time winner of The Mistress of the Darkpath

Connect with her online:

--Join my street team: facebook.com/TeamCharityParkerson
  --Website: charityparkerson.com
  --Facebook: facebook.com/authorCharityParkerson

facebook.com/TheMenofSin

--Twitter: twitter.com/CharityParkerso